Looking for a Waterhole

Colleen Rae

LOOKING FOR A WATERHOLE
© Colleen Rae, 2014
All rights reserved

Cover design:
SelfPubBookCovers.com/finecomm

Book design by Jo-Anne Rosen

ISBN: 978-1-941066-02-7

Wordrunner Press
Petaluma, California

Acknowledgments

*T*his story started in 1975 when I lived, worked, and played in Las Vegas. It is a work of fiction, and all of the characters are fictitious; however, I used many incidents that occurred during my time in Vegas in this novel.

I thank Guy Biederman of Marin County, California, an author in his own right and my mentor and novel workshop instructor extraordinaire, who critiqued *Looking for a Waterhole* in its roughest draft. Thanks to all of the various people in the novel workshop who added their suggestions. You know who you are.

Christie Nelson, author of *Woodacre* and *Dreaming Mill Valley*, and a dear friend, did me the honor of reading the book in its very basic form. I thank her for her good ideas, judgment, and for suggesting the title of this novel.

Grant Flint, author of *The Great American Novel; a Memoir*, and close friend, also read the entire novel recently and at an earlier time, and critiqued it with good ideas.

Thanks to Anne Fox of California Writers Club for her expert copyediting.

And also many thanks to JoAnne Rosen of Wordrunner Press, Petaluma, California, for all she did to bring this novel to print.

Las Vegas, in the 1970s, was like Snow White's poison apple; it could be fresh and beautiful on the outside, but underneath, deadly.

In 1975, the "Mob" still ran the casinos and hotels; the town had not yet become a family-oriented place as it is today. The entertainment was for adults, as was most everything in the town. The big shows advertised their dancers and showgirls as topless, as did all the bars, lounges, and smaller clubs. Against this backdrop, I show four women making their destiny in a town that was infamous for losers and addiction.

As the saying went, everyone in Las Vegas was either addicted to gambling, liquor, drugs, sex, or money.

For the wonderful man

in my life, Larry.

Contents

LOOKING FOR A WATERHOLE

A novel

by

Colleen Rae

Prologue
Raiatea, Tahiti, 1976

The woman on the beach was bathing in the sun. Wanda rolled over onto her stomach and felt the warm Tahitian breeze caress her back. Her breasts, nearly as brown as the rest of her, spilled onto a flowered blanket. A palm-thatched bungalow, ten yards away, huddled next to a steamy jungle. Mangos fell in soft heaps nearby, their rotting sweetness mixing with the magnificent aroma of tropical flowers. Gentle breezes carried the sweet scent of jasmine and plumeria cascading from the edge of trees. Wanda yawned. A chartreuse gecko with tiny red eyes darted toward the nearest palm tree for cover. Scalloped shore swept out like two white wings. Sultry blue waters lulled Wanda into sleepy contentment. Two miles out, a line of waves broke over a shallow coral reef. She removed sunglasses and straw hat and bunched her cotton *pareau* under her head. Her body glistened with Ban de Soliel, her red bikini bottom flashed in the noon sun. She stretched her legs, her pointed toes reminded her of how much she missed dancing. She hadn't danced since last year in Las Vegas.

Last year had been one long adventure. She began to remember it all: The people that were closest to her. Suzanne her roommate; Ruby, the stripper; Violet, the

1

waitress; her sisters, Iris and Naomi; Alan, Sol's nephew; and Sol, the only man she had ever loved.

Angel Moon
Las Vegas, 1975

*W*anda Moon, wearing only a G-string, tossed her T-strap across the stage. Breasts gyrating in opposition, brown nipples taut, she offered them to the audience. Shaking her shoulders, her breasts rocked gently from side to side. Remembering a line from an old song, *"Fat Miss Kelly wiggles just like jelly…"* made her smile.

A rotund man in the front row let out a howl. "Whoopee…!"

Another voice chanted, "Angel, Angel…"

Layered smoke drifted on currents of air-conditioning. Wanda wrinkled her nose at the gamey potpourri of day-old sweat and overworked sex glands. The music swelled to a crescendo as she strutted her last steps to Lou Rawls', "Walk on the Wild Side," hips and long black hair punctuating the music. High cheekbones and dusky skin proclaimed her ethnic origins. Wanda was a Chemehuevi Native American. She had grown up on the Colorado River Indian Reservation in Arizona. At seventeen, she ran away with a truck driver passing through. They stopped at Vegas for a cold drink, and he left her behind, figuring she could be real trouble for him. Next day, she got a job as a topless dancer, and after several months of studying the strippers, she worked up her own act. When she was a child her grandfather called her Little Flying Doe because she was always dancing and leaping across the ground. Now she was one of the headliners at the Arabesque Club, the classiest strip club in Las Vegas.

She exited the stage to catcalls, loud stomping, and clapping. As the curtain fell she scooped up her costume and walked gracefully on four-inch red heels to the dressing room. Passing Carmen, the exotic dancer going on stage, Wanda uttered, "Break a leg."

"Thanks," Carmen said over her shoulder.

In the dressing room, a beautiful redhead was sitting before a long mirror. She raised her eyes dramatically.

"God, Wanda," Candy said, "What'd you do out there?" She smoothed her fiery curls, talking and chewing gum simultaneously.

"Nothing different, just the usual bumps and grinds." Towel in hand, Wanda blotted her dark eyes carefully and wiped shimmering rivulets from her stomach. "Maybe they're all a little more shit-faced than usual." She tossed her costume on the back of a green upholstered chair and stashed her tips, four twenty dollar bills, in a side pocket of her purse.

She slipped into a cotton smock and pulled out a joint from her purse, lit it, and dropped her 5'8" frame into the chair. She draped one tapered brown leg over the arm, a red shoe balanced on the ball of her foot. Large breasts languished against her ribcage and peeked through the smock. She inhaled deeply and asked, "Want a toke?"

"You bet. I need to get stoned to get through my next set." Candy took the joint.

"You got the wrong attitude, honey." Wanda exhaled with a sigh. "What you got to do is feel empowered by your work on stage. For fifteen minutes you got their undivided attention. It's a challenge to see how long you can keep them enthralled. If anyone walks out during my act, I'm not doing my job."

Both women burst into laughter.

"Sure," Candy said. "Well, I have a hard time pretending. I always think of someplace I'd rather be."

She took another hit. "A tropical island or mountain cabin, instead of in front of a bunch of piranhas. By the way, Wanda, remember Star Ruby? She used to work here last year. Well, I saw her at Mr. Reeves, the other night. You know that dive downtown. She was on stage so fucked up, she was barely able to do her routine."

Wanda stared out the dressing room door. "Yeah, I remember her. God, that's too bad.

"She has a real problem with booze." She turned to look at the woman before the mirror. "What were you doing in that dive, Candy?"

Candy giggled. "I've been dating the manager, Matt. He pumps iron. You know how I love men that pump iron." She wiggled her eyebrows in her best Groucho impression.

Just then, Roxy the Fox and Peaches Canoe entered the dressing room. Rosy was a six foot blond with huge green eyes. Peaches was petite, strawberry blond, with a complexion to go with her name.

"Hey babes what's up, besides the ones out there?" Roxy smiled broadly.

"They're crazy wild tonight," Wanda replied. "Don't know what's going on."

"We practically got abducted at the stage door," Peaches said. "Not that I would have minded if I didn't have to work." She spoke in her best Georgia drawl.

Hal, the stage manager, stuck his head in the dressing room. "I want you to follow each other with no dead time on stage, tonight. Got it? We don't wanna' lose any of them. So pay attention. Carmen's just comin' off. Candy, you ready?"

The redhead nodded without enthusiasm.

Carmen pushed past Hal, costume trailing in one hand, dark hair sticking to glistening breasts. Hal never seemed to notice the bare bodies. He was all business. He was only interested in keeping the show going on time.

"The moon must be full or something," Carmen mumbled, "The animals are loose." She wiped her forehead with a towel.

"Oh, shit. Here I go." Arranging her boa around her shoulders, Candy glanced in the mirror one last time and then headed out the door.

Roxy and Peaches settled at the far end of the room, getting themselves ready.

Wanda offered the roach to Carmen. They heard the shouts and whistles as Candy took the stage.

Carmen took the joint between long, red fingernails, and put it to her lips, sucking in a whooshing sound to cool her mouth. She tossed it in the ashtray and threw herself down on the divan, stretching long legs.

"You know, Wanda, I've been thinking about shedding this town."

"Where would you go?"

"Maybe audition for one of those shows goin' on the road."

"Sounds like an interesting change." Traveling appealed to Wanda, too. One of these days she'd roam the world. She stretched out on the chaise lounge, letting her mind drift on the high. Roxy, and then Peaches, would do their numbers before she had to go on stage again.

Forty minutes later, Wanda began dressing for her next set. First, she donned her black leather Merry Widow, smoothing a black satin T-strap over her hips, and pulled on black mesh hose on her long legs hooking them to a black garter belt. She slipped her feet into black satin heels and placed a leather collar around her neck with a large silver buckle studded with rhinestones. Every piece was fastened with Velcro for easy removal. The last thing she took from her locker was a black sequined cat-o-nine tails.

Peaches came in, clutching a handful of bills, her creamy skin bathed in sparking droplets of moisture. "At least they're throwing money and not bottles."

As Wanda left the dressing room she heard the taped announcement. "And now, the beautiful, the sexy, the incomparable, Angel Moon." She strode toward the wings, snapping her whip like a disciple of the Marquis De Sade.

Star Ruby

*R*uby took one final look at her reflection in the dressing room mirror. She applied another black line beneath her lower lashes, gulped down the remainder of the whiskey in her glass, and took a last puff off her cigarette stub, just as Matt, the manager, stuck his head in the door.

"You're on next, Ruby. One minute."

She licked the tip of her finger and traced the little spit curls over each ear. Her frizzy, bleached-blond hair rose from her head like a windstorm. Rhinestone earrings dangled to her shoulders. Standing up on four-inch patent-leather platforms, she checked the blue sequined T-strap, running red fingernails across hip bones, making sure the Velcro was fastened, then down the crack between her cheeks, straightening the fabric. She threw on a see-through baby-doll nightie, and headed for the stage. She heard catcalls coming from the lounge. B.B. King's "Everyday I Have the Blues" came over the sound system. She slid between the curtains and began dancing. Spilled beer and stale cigarette smoke made her nose itch. She pinched away a sneeze. Her plump, kewpie-doll body swayed and gyrated as she moved sensually down the runway. A pole rose out of the floor of the stage. Ruby wrapped her legs around it and rode it like she would a man. Some of the customers were leering and smiling up at her glistening body. Her short, curvaceous legs opened to reveal a few curly dark hairs escaping the sequined costume.

A man down front shouted, "Hey, Ruby, do it baby."

She had worked at this club, Mr. Reeves, in downtown Vegas for three months. At times she almost forgot she had once been a headliner at the Arabesque Club. Star Ruby was her billing then. Sometimes she made a grand a week, including tips. She had owned a trunkful of sparkling costumes she shipped to Toronto regularly when she worked a club there. She couldn't recall where the trunk was now. The fog that had gradually enveloped her mind reminded her of the steam room at the gym back in the days when she could afford a membership. Sometimes, Ruby felt like a fragment of herself. As if she had misplaced part of who she was. It became increasingly difficult for her to come to work each night. She had to fortify herself with liquor before she could get it together to dress, get a cab and arrive at the club on time. The last time she was late, Matt said he would only give her one more chance.

Before coming to Mr. Reeves, she had worked a series of topless bars. In the middle of the night, she would wake up crying, fighting through webs of numbness, dreaming she had been fired again. She feared if she could no longer dance, she would have to work the streets. She'd known others who had gone that route. In the topless dancers world, that was absolute bottom.

She removed her bra and danced to the end of the runway. A big man with a large belly stood up and stuck a fiver in her hand. She began rotating her breasts so the tassels made perfect circles. Ruby gave him the usual business, a breast or two close to his face but was careful not to touch him. That was against the rules of the house as well as against the law. She didn't need any more trouble with the law. The last time she was busted for a DUI, her license was pulled. She'd spent a night in jail because she didn't want to call Violet, her roommate, to come and bail her out. She had to borrow money from Violet to pay the fine and then was ordered by the court to go to rehab for two months. A lot of good that did. She started drinking as soon as she got home each afternoon from rehab right up until she went on stage. Now, she had to commute to and from work in a taxi. That was expensive. Many nights, she barely made enough in tips to pay the cab fare.

Ruby heard the last refrains of the music. She grabbed the parts of her costume she had shed, left the stage, flung her arms in her wrap, and headed for the bar. Placing the five-dollar bill on the bar, she ordered a shot. Trembling, she anticipated the warm, burning whiskey sliding down her throat.

Alan

$\mathcal{A}$lan put the cards down, and stepped away from the 21 table to allow the new dealer to come on shift. He looked at his watch; 2:00 a.m. Leaving the Pit he nodded to a few of the other dealers on his way to the employees' back room. He dialed the combination of his locker to open it, hung up his apron, vest and tie, grabbed his shoulder pack and headed out to the bar. Climbing on a stool he spoke to Jake, the bartender.

"Give me the usual. What's up?"

"It's pretty slow. Not much action here. How about the tables?"

"Slow there, too. Well, it's Thursday. Usually quiet. Come tomorrow, the busloads arrive."

"Yeah, it'll be crazy, then."

Jake set a drink in front of Alan and moved down the bar to another customer. Alan lit up a Marlboro and took a healthy swig of his Glenlivet on the rocks.

Alan had arrived in Las Vegas after graduation from the University of Michigan. Back home in Bloomfield, when he announced he would not follow in the family waste-management business, his Uncle Sol offered him an opportunity in Las Vegas. Alan jumped at it. It sounded different and exciting. After dealers' school, Sol gave him the job in the casino of the El Morocco Hotel. It had been two years since Alan came to town, and he still found it the most exciting place he had ever been.

He finishing his drink and left a five on the bar. He waved at Jake, and headed out the employees' exit. The night was still warm. The day had hit 115 degrees, a typical summer day in Las Vegas. Moist, soft air caressed his skin. The heavy sweetness of tiger lilies wafted over the hotel wall. Alan wrinkled his nose at the acrid smell of chlorine drifting on lazy currents of air. He looked down the Strip. As far as he could see, billions of lights, all colors of the rainbow, embraced the black Nevada sky, like a light show on the fourth of July.

He cut across the parking lot to where his 55 T-Bird was parked. A tall blonde was struggling with her bags next to a green VW bug. He looked closely. She was one of the showgirls, Suzanne Cane. He'd noticed her the first time he saw the casino show, *Las Vegas Follies*. She was so poised and slim, small, perfectly shaped breasts with just the right amount of curves. All the showgirls wore huge headdresses, feathers, bangles and T-straps, but were topless. Because of her, he'd seen the show seven times.

She dropped one of the bags, keys rattling to the pavement. Alan passed his car and headed straight for her.

"Can I help? Looks like you need some." He scooped up the bag and keys. When he stood up, he looked into sky-blue eyes. Her naturally blonde hair hovered around her shoulders, like the feathered headdresses she wore on stage. She had removed the heavy makeup, and her skin glowed the color of honey. He thought she was even more beautiful up close.

"Thank you," she said softly. "Please, may I have my keys?" She seemed nervous, her voice trembling.

"Of course." He handed them to her. "Hey, don't worry. I work here, too. I'm a dealer. I know you're in the show."

She looked relieved. "Oh, good, I'm always a little frightened walking to my car at night." She unlocked her car door.

"I don't blame you." He held the door. "Why not ask the guard to walk you to your car? That's part of his job." Handing the bag to her, he added, "By the way, I'm Alan Wolfe."

"Hi. I'm Suzanne Cane, and that's a good idea. I'll do that from now on." She placed the bags in the passenger seat, climbed in, and slid her tanned legs under the wheel. "Thanks again for your help."

"You're welcome. See you around."

She smiled through the window, started her car, and drove out of the parking lot.

Alan walked to his own car, whistling a little nontune. He was thinking, wow, what a woman! He wondered if she had a boyfriend or was married. When he drove out of the lot, he saw her VW bug ahead. She turned right onto Paradise Boulevard, and he turned left. He waved, and she waved back. He would ask his Uncle Sol discreetly about her status. Sol had access to all the personnel records.

⌣

Alan parked in the two-car garage and entered his ranch-style house through the kitchen. Boots, his gray Persian greeted him, meowing for dinner. Reaching down, he stroked the cat behind the ears.

"My little pussy's hungry," he purred to Boots.

The cat purred back and stretched luxuriously, arching his back. Alan went to the refrigerator and took out a can of cat food, and emptied it into a bowl on the floor. Boots kept nudging his hand, licking the air with a pink tongue.

In the living room, Alan threw his shoulder pack on the chair. A large green couch stood against one wall, coffee table in front. An end table, a lamp, and a large overstuffed brown leather chair resided next to the couch. Stacks of old newspapers lay on the floor. Several pieces of clothing were thrown across the couch and chair. Dirty dishes on the coffee table had never made it to the kitchen sink. A cat-run extending from the floor to ceiling filled one end of the living room. Alan had built it himself. At the other end was a dining room table and four chairs. There were no curtains at the windows; only venetian blinds. They were always closed; the house existed in shadows, day and night. In a town where most everything was open all the time, Alan joined the ranks of those who found it difficult to identify when day stopped and night began.

He sat down, turned on a lamp, opened a Chinese porcelain box and took out a vial of white powder. He sprinkled a small amount on a mirror; took a razor blade, worked it into a line, then snorted it through a straw. A burning sensation permeated his nasal passages, as the bitter substance ran down his throat. Alan felt the familiar, euphoric rush. He visualized for a flash of a second that he was flying high above the buildings of downtown Las Vegas. Squeezing his nostrils, he cut off a sneeze.

Replacing the glass vial in the box, he moved quickly to the kitchen. He opened a drawer and took out two dozen Vicks inhalers. He filled a soup kettle with water, placed the inhalers in the pan, and turned on the burner. Standing before the stove, he thought of Suzanne seated on his green couch, her lovely body bare, her legs apart. He smiled and began assembling the various ingredients that went into the extremely dangerous recipe to create methamphetamine. On the street it was known as Speed.

Suzanne Cane

*S*uzanne pulled out into the Strip traffic, waving to the young man who had helped her. He seemed nice. She felt foolish that she had been frightened of him. His dark hair and dark eyes were exactly the kind of male looks she admired. But no, she didn't need a man in her life to complicate things. Her entire existence consisted of rehearsing four times a week, four dance classes, and six nights of performing. On her night off, Monday, she usually stayed home, did her laundry and wore no makeup. Her roommate, Wanda, was more social. Wanda always had a date or a new man in her life. Suzanne hadn't had a boyfriend for two years. In fact, the only men she even talked to outside of the dancers in the show were Wanda's friends, when she occasionally brought one home. Suzanne was obligated to go to the hotel parties after hours. Sometimes she had to perform there, too. She hated it and had discovered a way around the problem. If she acted drunk enough, the high rollers usually didn't insist she accompany them into a bedroom. This was part of her job as a showgirl. It had all been explained to her about three months after she'd started working in the show. They told her if she didn't want to entertain after hours, she wouldn't have a job. She agreed to do it because she liked the glamour and the money. But she couldn't take any pleasure in male company on her own time. She had turned down dozens of would-be suitors. Dating eventually led to sex. She didn't want to bed any more men.

Suzanne and Wanda

Suzanne turned into the gates of the condominium and parked in her space under the giant palm tree. Stepping from the car, she felt a breeze sway the palm fronds and cool her warm skin. She heard Wanda in the kitchen as she unlocked the front door.

"Hey, girl. How'd it go tonight?" Wanda took a package of tea from the cupboard.

"Okay. No after-hours parties. I'm home early." Suzanne threw her purse and bags on the table.

"So I see. Want a cup of tea?"

"Sure."

Wanda put the wet tea bag in a clean cup and poured boiling water over it. "The audience was weird tonight at the Arabesque Club. A guy tried to climb up on the runway, and the bouncier had to 86 him." She did a little dance step around the stove.

"God, don't you get turned off by all that stuff?" Suzanne grimaced.

"I guess I'm used to it," Wanda said as she poised on one foot. "I don't let it bother me. It's a job. A way to earn good money."

Suzanne looked sad. "I wish I didn't let it bother me."

"Honey, you just got to keep your mind on something else," Wanda said softly and handed her a cup of tea. "You could audition for the Arabesque. I'd help you get an act together. I don't have to sleep with anyone I don't want to. That's one of the nicest things about my gig."

Suzanne sipped her tea and was silent. Then she shook her head. "I'm so sick of this town, Wanda. I really want to leave. But I don't know where to go."

"You know, sometimes it's better to wait until you have a plan. Ever think about returning to Los Angeles, where your parents are?"

Suzanne rarely saw her parents these days. They were not understanding about her topless status. They never came to visit her, and she couldn't get time off from the show to go to California.

Suzanne looked at her roommate. "Would you go back to the reservation and live?"

Wanda laughed. "Good point, dear. Not on your life. There's nothing there for me. My father would probably marry me off faster than a rooster jumps a hen. No, thanks. I'm never going back." She didn't want to think about the guilt that suddenly billowed up inside.

"Do you ever hear from your family?" Suzanne asked.

"No. I don't want them to know where I am. They'd all be up here harassing me or getting into trouble. That's why I dance under the name Angel Moon, so no one knows who I am."

Suzanne envied and admired Wanda. Sometimes she wanted to disappear and become someone else.

Violet

$\mathcal{V}$iolet Kandinsky walked toward the conference room at the back of the casino, her tray laden with twelve drinks. Thick black curls hung heavy across her back. Violet-blue eyes had been the inspiration for her name. Her mother often said, "One day Violet's gorgeous eyes and good looks will take her out of this small Pennsylvania coal mining town." True to her mother's words, at eighteen, having saved enough money from her job at the drug store after school, Violet took matters into her own hands and purchased a bus ticket for as far as the money would take her. That was Las Vegas. She did try to keep in touch with her mother but wasn't very good about it. She never looked back.

Skillfully balancing the tray with one palm, she knocked once on the closed door that had no knob. It sprung open with a quiet click. Violet pushed against it with her shoulder and entered the room. Her eyes took a moment to adjust to the dark interior. The door swung shut as she stifled a cough with her free hand. Out of the corner of her eye, through the haze of cigarette and cigar smoke, she saw filmy shadows of suits and fedoras.

Carefully avoiding the eyes of the twelve men sitting around the table, she approached her boss, Nick Capela, setting a Scotch and soda in front of him, then proceeded to place a drink before each guest. As she passed each man they threw either a chip or a $20 bill on her tray. This was her tip; the drinks were comps.

She heard one man at the end of the table. "Nick, I like your help. Good looker."

Nick said nothing.

Keeping her head down, Violet heard someone else say, "Remember what I said, Nick. Bottom line is…you are responsible."

"Yeah, Ace. I hear ya'. I'm sure gonna' get on this, right away."

Another man with a deep voice spoke. "Now we aren't accusing anyone at this point. Just get a little undercover surveillance in place. If the cameras aren't showing anything, time to get some informants."

Violet finished the serving and headed toward the door. Nick pushed the invisible button and the door clicked open. She left as quietly as she had arrived, taking a deep breath as she stepped into the hallway. On her tray she counted $200. She slipped the tips behind her bank on the tray, the money with which she worked her shift.

Nick had interviewed her several months ago about serving his guests. He told her he would pay her an extra week's pay, and she didn't have to share her tips with Eddie, the bartender. Of course, she must never hear, see, or speak of anything that went on in that room.

She looked into Nick's Mediterranean brown eyes. With no hesitation, she said, "Of course, Mr. Capela. Thank you for the opportunity."

She had been serving Nick's guests for three months. This was the first time anyone noticed her. She would like to be invisible, if she had a choice. Better to go unnoticed in that room, unlike the casino, where the more attention she received, the more tips she made. She felt a strange thrill, knowing this was on the fringes of danger that fed her deep sense of adventure.

Violet checked in with Eddie at the bar. "I'm back. Want me to work the Pit now?"

Eddie had always been fair to Violet. She never shorted him his percentage of the tips. Some of the girls did, and they didn't last long.

"Yeah, cover Carol's tables," he said. "She's goin' on break." He brushed back his collar-length dark hair.

Because she was apparently trusted by Nick, Eddie treated Violet with more politeness than he did the other girls. Violet was one of the reliable waitresses, and soon after she started, Nick put her in charge of the shift schedules. She got extra money for that, too. It could be a headache at times. If one of the girls didn't show or called in sick, Violet had to find a substitute. Sometimes she couldn't find one and worried that Nick would be mad at her. Sometimes she would work a double shift to cover. Nick had told her several times she was doing a great job.

"Just keep up the good work," he'd said.

Violet hurried to the Pit, taking orders at the 21 tables. Above the casino, a small stage was suspended by cables for the ceiling. Marlena was doing her sensuous movements on the chaise lounge, taking positions like a calendar pinup. She was one of six dancers who did three shows a night for the customers.

When Violet returned to the bar, Eddie said, "Nick wants you to stay a few minutes after you finish your shift. He wants to talk to you."

"Sure." She avoided Eddie's stare. What did Nick want to talk to her about? She hadn't told anyone anything. Not even her roommate, Ruby. Ruby would be the last person to tell anything confidential. Alcohol was her main friend, and half the time she was in bed, passed out.

The rest of her shift went quickly. At 2:00 a.m. she served her last order. She gave Eddie his share of the tips, changed her working costume for shorts and tee shirt, packed up her things and headed for Nick's office. His door was ajar. She knocked softly.

"Come in, Violet."

She pushed the door open. He sat behind his wooden desk, feet propped on top, a cigarette in his left hand.

"Sit down."

She sat in the chair in front of the desk, crossing her long legs.

"I wanted to thank you for your work today in the back room. You remembered everyone's order perfectly."

She looked directly at him. "Thank you, Mr. Capela. I consider that just doing my job."

"Everyone thought you did that. By the way, I have a special job I would like you to do for me. And please call me Nick."

"All right."

He took his feet off the desk and leaned toward her. "When you are serving in the Pit, have you ever noticed any of the dealers or the bosses putting money from the tables anywhere but in the drop?"

Violet's heart lurched. "I don't know. I never pay any attention to that."

"From now on, I want you to pay attention. Not overtly, very carefully. Know what I mean?"

"I think so." Violet knew exactly what he meant.

"If you see anything that doesn't seem right, come and tell me. Will you do that?"

"Yes, Nick."

"I'll make this worth your while when I make out your paycheck."

"Thank you, sir."

"Please don't call me, sir," Nick said. "Around the others, you can call me sir."

"Okay, Nick."

He looked at her and smiled. "Have the guard at the back door walk you to your car."

"Goodnight." She smiled back and couldn't help noticing the lock of dark curly hair falling over his brow.

On her way out the back, she saw Phil, one of the security guards. "Phil. Nick said to walk me to my car."

"Sure thing, Violet. Make a lot of money tonight?"

Phil was trying to make conversation.

"Fair." Violet told no one what she made. She guessed the Eye in the Sky wasn't as efficient as she'd thought if Nick wanted her to do extra surveillance. Every casino had cameras hidden in the ceilings. All the employees knew this. Everyone was being watched at all times. So why would Nick want her to spy on the others? Someone was stealing, he practically said that. A vague feeling of anxiety almost canceled her excitement at working for him in this new capacity. She was entering dangerous territory. However, her love of adventure won out. She knew she felt stimulated when she was in Nick's presence. Cheeks flushed, violet eyes luminous, she got in her car, waved to Phil, the security guard, and drove out of the Calendar Club parking lot.

Sol

Sol Wolfe stepped from his silver Rolls Royce, handed the keys to the valet with a fifty-dollar bill.

"No scratches, son."

"No sir, Mr. Wolfe. I'll take good care of it."

He entered the Arabesque Club, found a seat near the front and ordered a Scotch rocks. He unwrapped a Havana and bit off the end and lit it. For ten years, he'd been coming here, enjoying the show and the girls. He liked the elegance of the red velvet chairs, the pretty waitresses, good service, and the cleanliness of the theater. Until recently, he had never been attracted to any of the strippers. But Angel Moon was different. When she came on stage, Sol experienced something he had never felt before. He wanted to meet her. Finally, after sitting through three dancers, B.B. King's, "The Thrill is Gone," poured over the sound system. Angel Moon strutted on stage, sequined costume flashing. Spotting Sol in the front row, she played just for him. First, she removed gloves, then feathered boa, slowly, tantalizing the audience in expectation. Next, offering a bare leg through a split in a long, silk skirt, and last, as if by magic the sequined bra suddenly appeared in her hand. Back arched, her large breasts stood straight up, rotating in rhythm of the music. Tassels attached to nipples twirled to perfect circles. By this time, Sol was completely enraptured. Nearing the end of her routine, Angel threw her T-strap in the air. It sailed in a perfect arc, landing in his lap. He felt sparks as if she had touched him. She took her bows, and picked up the money thrown on stage as the curtain closed.

Sol made a decision. He walked down the side aisle to the stage door, opened it, and was met by a security guard.

"I'm Sol Wolfe. I want to return Miss Moon's costume, and I'd like to meet her. Do you think you could arrange it?" A fifty-dollar bill appeared between Sol's fingers.

In one swift motion, the bill disappeared from Sol's hand into the guard's pocket. "I'll sure try, Mr. Wolfe," he said, as he hurried off toward the dressing rooms.

In a few minutes the guard returned. "Yes sir, Mr. Wolfe. Angel Moon said she'd be glad to meet you. Just give her a few minutes to change. Wait back there by the silver door."

He thanked the guard and stood outside the dressing room. In a few minutes the silver door opened. He was overwhelmed by her natural beauty. Jet black hair hung down her back, smooth and shiny. Thick brows crested dark brown eyes. She had taken off the red lipstick leaving her lips a soft pink. Turquoise Indian earrings hung from her earlobes. A long purple silk dress clung to her body. On her small feet she wore silver sandals.

"HI. I'm Wanda Moon." She held out her hand.

"I thought your name was Angel?" He grasped her small brown hand in his large one.

"Angel is my stage name. Wanda is my birth name. The name my grandfather, Walking Bear, gave me. I'm a Chemehuevi Indian."

"Yes, I know you're Native American. Of course Angel is your stage name." He'd spent too much time thinking of her as Angel. "Are all your people as beautiful as you?"

Wanda laughed. "No. We're just like everyone else. Some beautiful, some not. Our people have a saying — 'All beauty comes from spirit.'"

Sol nodded. "Yes. Not unlike my sentiments." He suddenly realized he hadn't introduced himself and was still holding her costume. "I'm Sol Wolfe. I wanted to return your costume personally. I've wanted to meet you for a long time."

"I confess, Sol, I've noticed you in the audience, for a long time, too." She smiled up at him, their eyes meeting in mutual admiration. Wanda tossed the garment through the doorway to a chair.

"Would you like to come have a drink with me? We could go to the Library Club for dinner if you like." The Library was an exclusive restaurant in which each booth was curtained for complete privacy. Many of the famous performers in Vegas went there after their own shows. A membership fee was necessary to belong to the club.

"I'd like that, Sol. Let me get my purse. I'll be right with you."

A warm, comfortable glow settled over Sol. He was finally going to spend some time with Wanda Moon.

He decided not to tell her his history and his family

origins yet. That could wait.

Sol's parents had emigrated from Hungary in 1939. They dropped the Stein from their name, Wolfestein, and became David and Miriam Wolfe. Settling in New York City, David continued to work as a tailor until he was able to bring his brother and family to the United States. The brothers moved to Detroit and started a waste-management business that made both families wealthy. Sol and his brother, Sid, continued to run the business after their father and uncle died. However, Sol was restless, and leaving the business in Sid's hands, he came to Las Vegas in the middle 1960s. He loved horse racing and prize fighting and made a fortune betting on both. This had enabled him to buy into several Las Vegas hotels. Along the way, he cultivated friends and contacts with the men who owned and operated the casinos. Sol made some powerful friends, and favors went both ways.

Wanda joined him, and they walked outside the club to his Rolls Royce. Tonight he would enjoy this beautiful woman's company and get to know her. He definitely wanted to have her in his life.

Nick Capela

$\mathcal{N}$ick locked his office door with the invisible button under his desk. He leaned back in his chair and daydreamed about Violet. She reminded him of his wife twenty years ago; before Lily became bloated from alcohol and Nick had to place her in an expensive sanitarium. Now, she had a serious psychosis and needed a full-time nurse after she'd tried to cut her wrists. It was costing him a great deal of money to provide the care, but he had no choice.

Violet's unusual eyes and dark hair was the exact coloring of Lily's before she'd decided to dye it a dull black. The whites of Lily's eyes had turned yellow, and the lovely violet color had faded to a watery blue. He shook his head as if to banish the memory of the woman his wife had become. It was partly his fault, he knew. After several years of trying, it became apparent they couldn't have children. He hadn't spent enough time with her, and she had never made friends in this town. After she began refusing him sex, he found other women to fulfill his needs. But they came and went, none of them meaning anything to him.

Violet was an anomaly among his female employees. Most of them didn't have a brain in their heads, were usually unreliable, and often tried to seduce him. He wanted to know Violet intimately. Years of making women his avocation warned him. Treat her like a lady. She would respond to that. He didn't know why he told her someone was stealing from the casino. The big bosses were breathing down his neck, and he had to find an excuse for the missing money. He needed a scapegoat for this, but he wasn't sure who it could be. He did want someone keeping an eye out on the dealers however, and this gave him a reason also to spend time with her.

The ringing of the phone interrupted his thoughts. He picked up the receiver and recognized the voice.

"Nick, Carlo here. The boys just returned, and Ace tells me you're puttin' some floor surveillance in place."

"Yeah, Carlo. Don't worry. I'll find where the money is going. Just a matter of time."

"Okay, but we don't have a lot of that. The other bosses are real upset. They figure about two mil has been skimmed already."

Nick sounded shocked. "My God! I didn't realize it amounted to that much. I can't believe one source is skimming all that cash." Nick wished he could have bitten off his tongue as the words slipped from his mouth.

"We can't either. Get busy, Nick. Find out where the money's goin.'"

"Right, Carlo. I'll do that." His hand shook as he hung up the phone. He felt cold and sweaty. When he wiped his brow, droplets fell on his Italian slacks. His gut was churning. No way he had skimmed that much. He figured he'd taken about $500,000 with the help of Tony Rivera, the accountant. Tony's share was half.

Remembering his wish of a minute ago, he wondered if Tony was skimming more. But when did he have the opportunity? Nick was with him every minute in the count room. He needed time to think this out and make a plan. He definitely needed a fall guy. He knew what would happen to whoever got the blame. Someone from back East would be sent out. And then that would be the end of it. Another body found in the desert or a headless body discovered in a cheap hotel room. Carlo's call reminded him that the New York bosses were getting anxious.

Nick remembered when he was a child, the Dons would gather for their afternoon socials on Prince Street in Little Italy. At that time, his father, Antonio Capela, was a small-time bookmaker. Antonio and his family had immigrated to the United States about the same time as several of the men who were now the owners of the Calendar Club. The Costo Nostro had given him a job as a bookie, and he had carefully paid his dues to the group. He made a good living for his family. In fact, Nick had gotten this job as casino manager because of his father's connections. But now he had possibly fucked up. He belched, tasting the bile rising in the back of his throat.

Ruby

Ruby reached for the Wild Turkey on the kitchen counter. She poured herself two fingers in a short glass. Hand trembling, she raised it to her unpainted lips and drank it all, then poured another shot. She lit a cigarette and carried the glass to her room. In the mirror, she saw blond hair with dark roots; face white and puffy. Dull gray eyes looked back. My God! When had she lost her looks? Ruby couldn't remember the last time she thought she was pretty. No one told her that anymore. She balanced the Marlboro, burning tip out, on the edge of the dresser and began applying makeup in preparation for the evening shift at Mr. Reeves. The mirror's reflection flashed a memory of a little girl, herself, peeking from behind a dressing partition, watching her mother make up her face, her mother getting ready for customers. Nylons and garter belt, strapless bra and red lipstick. Then later, from the single cot behind the partition, hearing the noises coming from the big bed across the room. The smacking of lips, the moaning and wheezing, the heavy breathing and sometimes cries. She thought they might be hurting her mother but was too scared to find out. She didn't know who her father was, but her mother implied it was Reverend Thorpe. He did give Ruby the money to leave Havens Hollow, Kentucky, after her mother's death. She wanted to get as far away from the memories as she possibly could, but too late, she realized they would never leave her.

When she arrived in Vegas, having a natural talent for stripping, she got a job at the Arabesque Club, the classiest club in town. She made excellent money, sewed her own beautiful costumes, and for a few years seemed to do okay. But gradually, the loneliness and self-loathing began to upstage her life.

She finished her makeup and drained the glass. Cigarette stubbed out, she headed for the kitchen and a refill. She told herself to slow down. There was still an eight-hour shift to work.

"Damn," she said aloud. "Ruby, you gotta' get it together." She filled a quarter of the glass and took a long swallow. The warm, amber liquid slipped smoothly down the back of her throat. She picked up the phone and dialed a number.

"Check Cab," said the voice at the other end.

"Please send #32 to the Desert Winds Apartments. Tell Craig it's Ruby. I need a ride to work."

"Sure thing, Ruby. It'll be there in fifteen minutes.'

Craig usually gave her a ride. Sometimes, if she didn't have the ten dollars for the ride home, he wouldn't charge her. A few times he had come in at her invitation, and they got it on for fifteen or twenty minutes. Then Craig had to get back to his job. That's all it really was to Ruby. Getting' it on.

In the kitchen, she swallowed the last of the whiskey, picked up her costume case, and headed for the door. She was sitting on the bottom of the stairs when Craig pulled up in his cab.

Suzanne and Alan

She looked at him over the rim of her pink champagne glass. They were having dinner in an expensive restaurant, The Chateau Vegas. Suzanne picked over her filet mignon. Alan had eaten every morsel of his. The white silk dress complimented her honey tan and her long golden hair glossy over one shoulder. This was their first date.

"Suzanne, have you ever married?" Alan asked from across the table.

"No."

"Have you ever been in love?"

She met his eyes. "No, I never have."

Alan shook his head. "I find that amazing. As beautiful as you are, you must have men always chasing you."

She looked down at her plate. "Not really. I've always been kind of shy. I was never popular in school."

"But your resume says you won several beauty contests in Southern California."

Suzanne looked surprised. "You've read my resume? How did you get to do that?"

Alan felt stupid. "I didn't read it, but I must admit I was so interested in meeting you that I asked my uncle to find out if you were married. He looked up your personnel file and discovered you were not. I'm sorry I upset you."

"Who is your uncle?"

"Sol Wolfe."

Suzanne had heard of Sol around the hotel. "I'm surprised that he could read my personnel file."

"My uncle's a stockholder in the hotel. He works in the Personnel Department and has access to all the files."

Quietly she said, "What else did he tell you about me?"

"Well, let's see. You grew up in Tarzana, California, and you're an only child. You were discovered working in a dress shop in the hotel by the choreographer. After that, you became on of the showgirls in the *Las Vegas Follies*."

Suzanne felt a surge of anger. "I'm not sure that your uncle has the right to divulge any information about me. I don't think it's proper."

"Hey, I'm sorry if I was out of line." Alan took her hand. "I just wanted desperately to find out if I could l call and ask you out. I didn't want a husband answering the phone. Okay?"

He smiled, and his entire face lit up.

What he said did make sense, Suzanne thought. And he did have a wonderful smile. Relenting, she said, "Okay."

"Do you like working as a showgirl?" Alan asked, to change the subject.

Suzanne's face changed and became shadowed. "Sometimes. I like the dancing and being on stage. But I don't like to have to go to after-hour parties. The big boss at the theater says we all have to go."

Alan made a mental note to talk to Sol about that. "Guess being a showgirl isn't all glamour and fun," Alan said.

Suzanne shook her head.

She looked so sad suddenly that Alan tried to cheer her up. "Hey, let's get out of here. We could drive up to Sunrise Mountain. The moon is full, and it's a beautiful drive."

She smiled, but said nothing.

Alan paid the bill, and they left the restaurant.

Conflicting emotions swirled in Suzanne's head. She felt very attracted to this charming man. He'd been persistent and in a moment of weakness she agreed to go out with him. But she was afraid, too. Outside, the sweet aroma of jasmine and gardenias drifting on the evening breeze reminded her of an old adage of her mother's: a jasmine bush outside your bedroom window guarantees a happy marriage bed.

Violet

$\mathcal{H}$er shift over, Violet walked toward the back exit, heels clicking on the tile floor. Passing Nick's office door, partly open, she noticed a light inside. She continued down the hall.

"Violet, could you come into my office for a minute?"

Turning, she saw Nick standing in the hallway. She saw his dark eyes, like banked coals. His tousled hair fell in deep waves. He looked as if he needed a good night's sleep. She followed him inside, and he closed the door.

"Have a seat." She sat down facing the desk. Nick pulled his soft leather chair out and threw himself down.

"Have you noticed anything unusual in the Pit?"

Violet swallowed before she spoke. "No, Nick. I've seen nothing out of the ordinary. The Pit Bosses watch everyone closely."

"I'm going to take you into my confidence. Someone is definitely skimming in the casino. I need to find the guilty party."

Violet's eyes widened. "I understand. I'll do whatever I can to help. But I just haven't seen anything." She brushed a lock of hair over her shoulder. My God! This was serious business for Nick. She had thought it was just a dealer holding back a few hundred dollars a night.

Nick looked up and smiled, his entire demeanor changed. "Would you care to come to the Library Club with me and have a late dinner? I would very much like your company."

She knew immediately she would go, even though he was married. Even though all the rules say you don't fraternize with the boss. She'd never been inside the Library Club. It was out of her league. "Yes, thank you."

Nick came from behind the desk and grabbed his jacket from the coat rack. Brushing shoulders, the static electricity between them snapped in the dry room, sending a flash of pain down Violet's arm. They both jumped and then laughed.

Fortunately, she had worn heels and a nice mini dress to work so she looked presentable. She picked up her sweater, and he locked the office door and took her hand, his strong grip warm and soothing to her cool fingers. They headed toward the back exit. They barely spoke on the way to the restaurant. He offered his arm as they entered the golden double doors. The maître d' immediately welcomed them.

"Good evening, Mr. Capela. Right this way, please."

They were led to a curtained booth at the back. Violet noticed a lovely dark-haired woman with a silver-haired man slipping into the booth next to them. She recognized Angel Moon from her photos in the paper. The women exchanged smiles. When the maitre d' pulled the green satin drapes back, Violet saw a cozy table set for two with white tablecloth and white napkins. Pink roses on the table spread their seductive scent. The only light came from two elegant candles on the table. A long, plush seat with padded back beckoned. Two shelves of books filled the far end of the alcove. As if anyone would consider reading in this setting.

Eddie

*E*ddie scanned the interior of the casino. He could see most of it from his station at the bar. Carole, Violet, and Sharon were working the Pit. Beverly, Lynne, and the three new girls were in the slots. The casino was busy tonight. One of the performers, Marilyn, was doing her nightly couch routine on the suspended stage. They all left him cold. Now, the waitress with the purple eyes, she was something else. But she had already attracted Nick's attention. Eddie had a sweet thing going here. A good job with lots of opportunities. No use fuckin' it up for a broad. Just as he was fantasizing Violet in his power, she materialized at the bar.

"Need three Scotch rocks, one shot Old Taylor, two Gin tonics, and one Stinger," Violet read from her pad.

Eddie was already pouring the drinks before the last words left her mouth. He hoped the counter hid the swelling beneath his fly. "Whoever's drinkin' this Stinger will leave his money at the table. Guaranteed."

Violet nodded. "No doubt. He's already smashed." She picked up the drinks and placed them on her tray.

Eddie watched her walk toward the Pit, hips sway-ing in the short black costume, long legs sheathed in black mesh hose. It was a damn shame he couldn't have any of that.

He saw her serve the Pit customers and glance up at the Pit Boss now and then. Was she interested in him? He was married and not known for dating any of the waitresses. But then anything could happen. One never knew who was sleeping with whom around here. The sex gossip was fast and furious.

His gaze followed Violet as she made her way to the last table that had new customers, took orders, then back she came to the bar.

"What's going on with the Pit Boss down there? You got a hot date tonight?" He deliberately tried to throw her a curve.

Violet's Mediterranean complexion reddened. "Uh…no, Eddie. Just looking around."

He must have been watching her. He saw her glance at the Pit Boss. She was just following Nick's orders, but she couldn't share them with Eddie. She'd have to be more careful, looking and watching.

Wanda

Wanda entered the dressing room, blotting her makeup with a towel. She stretched out on the chaise lounge, and wiped down her perspiring body.

"You on soon, Roxy?" She glanced over at the stripper examining herself in the mirror, smoking a cigarette in a golden holder, fingers gripping it like she was playing a flute.

"Yeah, pretty soon." Roxy continued to examine her face, running long nails across eyebrows, along cheekbones, trailing her fingers over full lips, and down her throat, caressing the curve of one ample breast encased in a bra. Her long flowing skirt had pink feathers, as did her headpiece. The headpiece hung halfway down her back, covering long, blond hair. A large yellow beak extended over her forehead. She resembled an exotic bird, hovering, about to take flight.

"Can you see the scars, Wanda?" Roxy asked.

"Sure can't." Wanda was fanning herself now with a hand-painted Chinese fan.

"The plastic surgeon, he was a miracle worker," Roxy said. "He practically molded me a new face. And he removed every whisker, as well." Her large blue eyes heavy with artificial lashes winked at Wanda. A feminine smile lit up her face. "Can you imagine what the guys out front would do if they knew I was born a man?" Tickled at the thought, Roxy gave a low chuckle, separated the cigarette from its holder, and twisted it in the ashtray.

Wanda leaned toward her and spoke softly. "You know, I've heard a rumor that the management put a bug in our dressing rooms. I'd be careful what I say if I were you."

"Hey, I don't give a fuck if they find out. I'm proud of my trans-job. It sure would give ol' Richie a heart attack, though. I've fucked him more than once." She spoke loudly in case there *was* a mike backstage. Richie Abrams was their boss. He owned the Arabesque Club. Or so everyone thought. Ownership in Vegas could be a murky subject. "Are your ears burnin', Richie?" Roxy rocked with laughter.

"Don't you care about your gig? He might fire you." Wanda stood and changed into a caftan.

"I don't think he'd fire me. As long as the patrons out front don't know. I got a reputation as a damn good stripper in this town. The management has some investment tied up in all of us. It wouldn't do them any good for the public to find out they've been employing a sex-change stripper all these months. Besides, Richie really gets off on my bod. I think he'd still want some more action." Roxy roared again.

"I'd just be careful. You don't have to make these people mad at you. You never know who you're dealing with, know what I mean?" Wanda's voice got considerably lower at the last sentence.

"Yeah, Wanda, I know what you mean. But I'm not

running scared. I've advanced my career from a horizontal position. Too many guys in this town would be real embarrassed to find out they fucked a transsexual!" Roxy fluttered her lashes at Wanda.

"I swear, you're incorrigible," Wanda said. "Well, try to stay out of trouble, girl. I gotta' get ready for my next set." Still laughing, Wanda sat down at the mirror to repair her makeup.

Roxy stood, six feet tall, tossing the tail feathers of her costume behind her. "Did you know I have an identical twin brother? Of course, we aren't identical anymore. He lives in San Diego. He's a real tennis jock. I never see him, anymore. I think he's more embarrassed than anyone in my family. I really miss the guy."

Hal, the stage manager, craned his head in the door. "Roxy, you're on in one minute."

"Coming, Hal."

"Break a leg, Roxy," Wanda said.

"Right, girl." Roxy gave herself one last admiring glance in the mirror and carried her extraordinary body out of the dressing room. Wanda could hear the cheers and shouts of "Roxy, Roxy" from the audience, as she went on stage.

Nick and Violet

*N*ick drove the Cadillac through the gates of the Las Vegas Country Club Estates. On each side of the street Violet saw mansions with circular drives and lush, manicured grounds. He pulled into the drive of a three-story adobe house with a turret on each end. When he unlocked the front door, the first thing she saw was a statue of an ancient goddess, nestled against the opposite wall—thick torso and broken arms raised in silent tribute. Beyond, a white circular staircase swept to a glass-domed ceiling three floors up.

She followed Nick into the main room. Primitive masks adorned white walls, exotic spears resting beside them. The furniture was entirely white, and the wall-to-wall carpeting was thick white pile. Full-length windows overlooked the golf course. African and Middle Eastern artifacts, Etruscan pottery and clay statues, stood on low tables, their ancientness in sharp contrast to the modern furnishings.

"It's beautiful, Nick." Violet had seen such affluence only in the movies. She walked to the windows. Large palms backlit by flood lights cast shadows across the edges of the eighth hole. She gazed around Nick's house taking everything in.

"This is where I put my VIPs if they don't want to stay in a hotel. Sometimes my guests want to keep a low profile. But they only come every few months."

Violet nodded, still in awe at the luxury of Nick's home. "Have you traveled and collected all of these things?"

Nick laughed. "No, honey, I inherited this place from its former owner. That's another story. He ended up going to jail, so I bought the house and everything in it." He came up behind her, slipping his arms around her waist. The aroma of expensive Italian aftershave enveloped her.

"This will be our place," he said. He turned her around and kissed her long and hard, sucking her lips into his mouth. She pressed against him, feeling his hardness. He ran his tongue along the side of her neck and down the base of her throat and kissed her shoulders. Taking her hand, he led her up the circular staircase to a bedroom. He gently pushed her down on the white satin bed and removed her blouse, then slipped her slacks over slim hips and tore away her panties. Skillfully shedding his own clothes, he lay down beside her and kissed her breasts, her eyes, and her mouth. Violet couldn't remember feeling this kind of intense passion before. Their bodies burning, they rubbed and slid against each other. When she came against his mouth, she cried out his name. He entered her and immediately climaxed.

After they rested, it began all over again. Their hunger for each other took a long time to sate. Gray light filtered through partially open blinds when Violet finally fell asleep. She was completely at peace, refusing to think of a future or the almost certainty that they did not have one together.

Alan and Suzanne

Alan drove into his garage and glanced over at Suzanne. She was quiet, her eyes turned away. He got out and walked around to her door.

Unwinding her long legs, she stepped from the car. His arm encircled her waist as he caught her special scent of baby powder and jasmine. He laid his lips on her temple, feeling her pulse flutter against his mouth.

"Let's go in. I need to check on dinner," he said, trying to maintain a lightness. His hunger threatened to overpower him. He led her into the house through the garage door.

Last week he'd decided to invite her for dinner at his house. He'd put away all the drug paraphernalia and hired professionals to come in and clean. They were instructed to do the stove very carefully. The cat was put outside while the rugs were cleaned. After the cleaners left, Boots, the cat checked out everything, smelling each corner, like he expected some foreign animal to surface.

In an attempt to make the place more presentable, Alan had bought a few things; four long-stemmed wine glasses, blue cloth napkins, and placemats for the dining room table. A few pillows for the living room, and a sea green chenille spread to go with the green curtains in the bedroom, hoping he might get lucky.

Suzanne felt tense as she entered the kitchen. She feared she could not fulfill what Alan had in mind. The first thing she experienced was a soft furry ball wrap around her ankle. She looked down and saw Boot's huge green eyes starring up.

"What an adorable cat, Alan. You didn't tell me you had a cat. What's its name? Is it a male?"

"Boots," Alan replied. "He's kind of male. I had him fixed. He's good company when I come home from work in the middle of the night."

Suzanne crouched down and slid her hand over the silky fur. Immediately Boots began to purr.

"Sweet Boots," she cooed as the cat took possession of her foot.

"Ease up, cat. I saw her first." Alan gently nudged Boots with his shoe.

Suzanne laughed a high, tinkling sound that reminded him of chimes in the wind. They went into the living room and he gestured toward the couch.

"Have a seat. I'll open the wine."

She sat down and leaned back against one of the new pillows. Noticing the large cat walk at the other end of the room, she figured Alan thought a lot of his pet. The dining table was attractively set with blue dishes, and she could see a flash of green spread beyond the open bedroom door. Not bad for a bachelor.

Alan returned with two glasses of Chianti Classico. "We're having Italian tonight," he said, "so I thought this wine would be nice."

"Here's to new friends," he said, looking into her eyes.

She held his gaze for a few seconds and then looked away. "Yes, this is nice wine," she said, enjoying the tartness on her tongue.

"For the main course, we are having eggplant parmangiana, a Caesar salad, which is my specialty, and pineapple upside-down cake for dessert."

"For heaven's sake, Alan, did you cook this all yourself?"

"Yes, my dear. Cooking is one of my hobbies. I'll make some woman a very nice husband." He grinned as he placed two salads on the table.

⤸

Alan cleared the dishes and sat down next to Suzanne on the couch. Boots was curled up at her side, Suzanne's hand resting on his head.

"My cat certainly approves of you. Boots doesn't like just anyone. Do you know you are the first woman ever to have dinner in this house?"

Suzanne was surprised. "Really? I'm flattered."

"I don't bring many people home. I have a couple of friends who watch football games with me on weekends. That's about it," he lied.

"Thank you for the delicious dinner. I'm afraid I can't cook a meal like that."

"I'll certainly lend my taste buds for anything you want to whip together."

"Is that your way of wangling an invitation to dinner at my house?"

"Whatever it takes." He reached over, took her hand, and gently kissed her lips. Opening his mouth slightly, he barely brushed her bottom lip with his tongue. She shivered in his arms. The kiss became more intense as he tightened his embrace. He wanted to crush her in his arms, but he didn't. Sensing she was hesitant, even a little frightened, he decided not to try to make love to her this time.

Suzanne pulled away. "It's time I went home. I have a rehearsal tomorrow before the show, and I need to get a good night's sleep." Her throat had a husky quality that she didn't recognize.

Alan stood, straightening his pants. "All right, my dear, I'll drive you home. Boots and I are sorry to see you go but hope that you will be back, soon."

Suzanne couldn't trust her voice at that moment, so she smiled. Walking to Alan's car, she guessed his Uncle Sol hadn't told him everything in her personnel file.

Wanda and Sol

On their fifth evening together, Wanda surprised Sol by accepting an invitation to his penthouse. After they exited the elevator, Sol unlocked a white double door, and Wanda entered a foyer that opened onto a huge living room with glass on three sides, overlooking Las Vegas. She stepped to the wall of windows. The entire Strip was visible to the north. Multicolored lights blinked and sparkled their magic across the town. Beige Scandinavian furniture gave the room lots of space. A red and blue Matisse and a still life by Cezanne hung over a white marble bar. She stared at the Impressionist paintings.

"My God, Sol, those paintings look like originals! They must have cost a fortune."

He nodded.

"You haven't leveled with me. Something more than 'Personnel Boss' in your title?"

Sol walked behind the bar and placed a record on the turntable. "Well, yes. I'm a stockholder also in the El Morocco. And I have stock in a couple of other hotels." Carl Orff's earthy *Carmina Burana* resonated softly from the stereo, beginning its long, slow build.

"Here I thought you'd rented the Rolls just to take me out."

"No, it's mine. Would you like a drink, honey?"

Wanda squinted her eyes. "So you don't *have* to work at the casino. Why do you?"

Sol took a bottle of Glenfiddich from the freezer and poured himself a generous amount. "I like to work there. It makes me happy." He gave her a big grin.

She shook her head. "Wouldn't you rather be on the golf course?"

"No." He smiled again. "Want a drink?"

"Scotch, please, on the rocks." Wanda walked over to the spotless sofa, sat down, and gently caressed the cushions. "Well, if I had a ton of money, as you obviously do, I'd leave this town and be on my way to Tahiti."

Sol looked at her over the rim of his glass. "Would you want to come back to Vegas?"

"Depends on whom I'm with," She looked up at him and smiled.

He set her drink on the teak coffee table. "Maybe we'll just go to Tahiti one of these days. Would you like that?" He joined her on the sofa.

Wanda met his eyes. "I have a contract at the Arabesque. I'm committed to work six nights a week for another six months."

"A lot of things can happen in six months, my dear." He took her hand and kissed her fingers. His lips found her mouth. At first, he kissed her gently, then with more insistence, exploring the soft interior with his tongue. His hands found her breasts. By now, the music had escalated to a fervent cadence, heightening their awareness with each repetition of the primitive chanting. While the monks in *Carmina Burana* celebrated

their bawdiness, Wanda and Sol surrendered to their
own sensuality.

"Come with me." Arm around Wanda's waist, he
led her to the bedroom. He threw off the green satin
spread and tossed it to the floor.

She kissed him, her full lips open. She slipped off
his shirt and unbuckled his belt, struggling with the
zipper against his hardness.

Wanda's flesh felt hot as he slid pink panties down
her brown legs. With his mouth on her breast, their
limbs entwined, he felt the music of her heartbeat.

There was a gentleness about this man mixed with
an intensity that she'd never experienced before. She
had slept with many men, but this man was giving her
something she desired besides sex.

In Sol's fifty-five years he had learned a few things
about women. He pleasured Wanda in the way that all
women love.

"Oh yes," she murmured, hips rocking to her own
inner rhythm. Wanda came as the crashing of symbols
proclaimed the music's joyful conclusion. She came
again, as Sol plunged inside.

His arm beneath her black hair, Sol knew this was
different.

Suzanne

Suzanne gulped down her martini. Across the room, one of her fellow dancers linked arms with a dark-skinned man in Arab dress and headed to one of the bedrooms in the back of the suite.

The balding man sitting beside her said, "Want a drink?" He put his hand on her knee, mini-skirt resting at the middle of her thigh. Suzanne nodded, and the man motioned the bartender to bring them another. The bartender quickly served Suzanne's martini and a Scotch rocks for the high roller. She gripped the stem of the glass, and took a long swallow, white knuckles against her tanned hand.

"Let's go back. I want to get started." The man laid his hand possessively on her arm.

Suzanne shuddered and staggered slightly when she stood. He tightened his grip.

He steered her along the hallway. They stopped at the first door and opened it. A nude couple was on the bed, rocking back and forth. He shut the door and continued on down the hall. At the end, he saw a vacant room and pulled Suzanne into it, closing the door. He took the empty glass from her and placed it on a table. He gently pushed her onto the bed and removed his tie. Suzanne watched with glazed eyes as he continued to undress. When he got to his boxers, he looked down at her and said, "Undress."

Suzanne automatically removed her dress, bra, and bikini underwear. He lowered himself on top and began kissing her mouth, breathing in heavy puffs. He snorted on her neck and then drooled over one shoulder to her breast.

She had always wanted to be a dancer. If doing this enabled her to keep her job in the show, she would get through it somehow. Just lay quietly, she told herself. It would all be over soon.

She remained quite still, her arms at her sides. When he took her nipple between his teeth and bit the tip, she jerked in pain.

"Did that feel good, honey? Come on, get down there and do it." He sat up, his penis huge, blood-purple, quivering in expectation.

Suzanne looked down and shuddered but didn't move.

Losing patience, he pressed her legs open with his hip and plunged inside.

Suzanne winced and cried out.

"Hey, you like that." Immediately he started pumping, riding her to a quick finish. "Yeah, baby," he said, as he came, humping her deeper.

Suzanne cried out again.

He let his whole weight sag onto her slim frame. His strong odor, gamey from exploding testosterone, made her stomach lurch. Finally, he pushed himself up and climbed off.

"I figured you'd warm up eventually. Now that wasn't so bad, was it, baby?"

"It was fine," Suzanne murmured. She slide from the bed and went to the bathroom. She cleaned herself at the sink, returned to the bedroom and put on her clothes. Immediately, she left the room, picking up the C-note on her way out. She scooped up her shoes and purse in the living room and left the suite. Leaning against the walls of the elevator, her head spinning, she slipped her bare feet into the shoes. In the parking lot she stood between two cars and vomited the martinis, splashing her new beige pumps. Her long fine hair caught at the corners of her mouth. She clung to the car for several minutes, trying to control the dry heaves and sobs that racked her body. Finally, she found her VW, climbed in, and headed home.

Ruby

*T*he yellow cab stopped at the curb in front of Mr. Reeves Topless Club. A group of people were looking at something on the sidewalk. When they thinned out, Craig could see a woman lying on the ground, her skirt hiked up to her hips, short legs bunched in a fetal position, blond head hanging over the curb.

He jumped from the cab, recognizing Ruby. "Get back, everybody. Give me some room." He knelt down, and picked her up in his arms. She seemed light in spite of her plumpness. He struggled to a standing position, and one-handed, opened the back door of his cab, and slid her in. The curious bystanders moved on, no longer interested in a drunken woman passed out on the street.

Craig locked the doors of the cab and went into the club. Matt, the manager and bartender tonight, was pouring drinks. A few men were still at the bar, watching a skinny blond gyrate to Neil Diamond's "*Mandy*."

"What the hell happened to Ruby?" Craig demanded. "She was on the street passed out!"

"She got snockered tonight," Matt said, "couldn't go on, so I fired her. I gave her plenty of warning. I can't run a topless joint with drunken dancers."

"Did you pay her for her time this week?"

Matt looked away. "No, I haven't yet."

"You can give it to me. I'm taking her home." Craig waited.

Matt hesitated, then went to the till, took out some bills and handed them to Craig. "She worked four nights. Here's a hundred."

Craig didn't even bother to thank him. He strode out to the cab, got in and drove away, tires squealing. Damn Ruby! Why couldn't she get a grip on herself? He knew the answer. She needed help. Like he had gotten years ago.

He drove to Ruby's apartment, found her key in the costume bag, and carried her in. He placed her none too gently on the couch.

Ruby stirred. "What the...hell? Wha's happenin'?" She opened blurry eyes.

"It's me, Craig. I brought you home. You passed out on the sidewalk." His voice was gruff.

"Oh, Craig, I don't remember leavin'," Ruby said, rubbing her eyes. Black smudges appeared on her cheeks.

"Matt fired you. You couldn't keep it together tonight. What the hell's the matter with you? Don't you care about anything anymore?"

Ruby was silent. Then the tears slowly slipped down her cheeks, mixing with the mascara. "I don't know. I can't remember."

Craig immediately felt sorry that he bawled her out. No use trying to reason with a drunk.

"I got your pay for you." He laid the bills on the coffee table. "I'm gonna' run a bath. You smell awful. Did you throw up?"

Ruby nodded, tears still flowing. He stared at her for a minute then went in the bathroom and started the water in the tub. When it was full, he returned to the living room and undressed her.

She gave him a half smile. "Thanks, Craig, for bringing me home."

He said nothing.

He sat in the living room while Ruby washed, and when she was drying off he rummaged through her dresser for a nightgown. "For Christ sake, where do you keep your nightie?" he called out to her.

She giggled. "I don't have one. I sleep in the nude."

He grabbed a large tee shirt and returned to the bathroom. He tugged it over her head. She leaned on him as he led her to the bed. He tossed back the unmade covers and Ruby slid in. He tucked the blanket under her chin, and gave her a peck on the cheek.

"Now you get a good night's sleep. I'll be back tomorrow around 6 p.m. See if you can leave the booze alone tomorrow. We're going to a meeting."

"What meeting?"

"You'll see tomorrow night. I gotta' go finish my shift."

Craig went into the kitchen, found the Wild Turkey and dumped it down the drain. He carried the empty bottle with him, slammed the door and locked it.

Ruby felt a giant headache beginning. She reached for the aspirin beside her and took four with several gulps of water. Craig sure sounded mad. But he did seem to care what happened to her. That never occurred to her before. Just when she thought she needed another drink, she drifted off to sleep.

Violet and Ruby

*T*he morning was already half over when Violet left Nick's apartment for home. He had gone out around nine for an important appointment. Breakfast had been sent in by the nearby café and they sat at the table in front of the full-length windows overlooking the Strip, sipping coffee, enjoying the Eggs Benedict, hash browns and toast. Nick playing toesies with her under the glass table. She watched the progress of his feet moving toward hers. Even this gave her a thrill in the pit of her stomach. He handed her a key and said he would tell her when the apartment was empty for them to use it. Meanwhile, she could bring clothes over and leave them in the master bedroom closet.

Nick had dressed and gone to an appointment, and after taking a luxurious bath in the Jacuzzi, Violet dressed and drove home.

The first thing Violet saw when she opened her front door was the money on the coffee table. A roll of twenties which must be Ruby's. She picked up the bills and quietly walked to Ruby's room. Ruby's blond head was nearly obscured by the blanket. Violet tip-toed into the room and laid the money on the dresser. Ruby opened her eyes as Violet was moving toward the door.

"Hi, what time is it?" Ruby rubbed her eyes. "I had the strangest dream."

Violet looked at her watch. "It's 10:30 a.m. What kind of dream?"

"I dreamed I got fired from Mr. Reeves, and Craig carried me home in his arms."

"That is a bad dream. At least the first part. I put your cash on the dresser. You left it on the coffee table." Violet exited the room.

She heard a faint "Thanks," as she walked down the hall. She ground some coffee and started the coffeemaker for Ruby, who always drank two or three cups of coffee in the morning to jump-start her day. Afterwards, in her bedroom, Violet sprawled across her purple bedspread, musing on her evening with Nick. She was definitely in love. She had never had a man treat her way Nick did. He said he wanted to buy her a diamond ring to show everyone she was his. But Nick had a wife, and even though she was in a sanitarium, he was married.

She heard Ruby puttering around in the kitchen. She changed into her housecoat and joined her.

Ruby was sitting at the kitchen table, holding her head in her hands. A freshly poured cup of coffee was in front of her on the table.

"I don't think it was a dream, Violet. I think I really got fired."

Violet poured herself a cup. "Why do you think that?"

"I remember Craig telling me last night after he put me to bed that I had been fired by Matt. He said I got drunk and couldn't dance."

Violet was silent. She knew Ruby went on binges, but mostly she just had several drinks to get her through the night.

"I think I've really fucked up this time. I don't know where I'm gonna' get another job. Don't know how I'll make my share of the rent next month." Ruby looked up at Violet, her eyes bloodshot and vulnerable.

"Don't worry about next month. I can cover it for us both. But the following month I'm not sure. Hopefully you will have another job by then." Nick had said if she needed money for anything, she was to ask him for it and he would give it to her.

"Thanks, hon." Ruby said as she started to cry. "I don't know what to do. I've worked at all the topless joints and been fired from most. I can't think of one that would hire me back." Tears rolled down her pale cheeks.

Violet grabbed a tissue from the counter and handed it to Ruby. "Don't cry, honey. It will work out. You'll see. I can pay our rent and buy food for quite a while. You're not to worry. But Ruby, you do need to get some help. You're drinking far too much."

Ruby took offense at Violet's criticism. "I don't drink anymore than anyone else in this town. Everyone drinks. I just need to cut back a little. Just so I can maintain."

Violet had told her before that she needed help. It hadn't penetrated Ruby's defensives. "You need to cut back a lot and get some rest. Then in a few weeks you can look for another job. Ruby, you don't have to work in a topless club. You could do something else."

Ruby looked at Violet, her eyes wide. "What else could I do? I don't know how to do anything but dance."

"You're a fine seamstress," Violet reminded her. "I've seen your costumes that you made when you were a stripper at the Club Arabesque. You could get a job as a seamstress for any show in Las Vegas. They always need talented people to make and repair costumes. It pays very well, too. It's a union job, and they make sure their workers get a good salary."

"I couldn't afford to join any union. I have no money, Violet. I haven't saved a penny."

"We'll worry about that when the time comes. Right now, I want you to concentrate on staying sober and getting lots of rest. I'll inquire what shows are hiring seamstresses."

"You're awfully good to me. I don't know what I'd do without a friend like you. You know, Craig is a friend, too. He brought me home last night, put me in the tub and then to bed and didn't even try to fuck me." Ruby giggled.

"That is a surprise, a man not trying to fuck a defenseless woman." Violet made a face and hammed it up. "Maybe there's hope for mankind after all."

"It surprised the hell out of me, too," Ruby admitted. In fact, she was just a bit disappointed that Craig didn't want to have sex with her. He hadn't made a move on her in months.

Violet stood, "I didn't get a whole lot of sleep last night. Why don't you take it easy and stay in today?

Watch T.V. I'll see you later this afternoon. I'm going to sleep four or five hours before work."

"What kept you awake all night?" Ruby asked.

"I'll tell you later. Right now, I need my sleep." Violet yawned and headed for her bedroom.

As soon as Ruby heard the bedroom door shut, she got up and opened the nearest cupboard, then the next and the next. She moved every can and package on the shelves but couldn't find the Wild Turkey. "Damn. Must have drank it all," she murmured. She thought she had another bottle stashed somewhere, but she couldn't remember where. "Damn," she said again, remembering Craig's instructions not to drink before he came to pick her up at six.

Sol

"*H*aven't seen you in a while, what have you been up to?" Sol and his nephew, Alan, were having a drink in the Polynesian Room after work.

"I've met a girl. I think I'm in love." Alan sipped his Scotch with a big grin on his face.

"Think you're in love. Don't you know?" His uncle settled back in the wide booth, puffing on a Havana.

"I'm sure, but she isn't yet. I mean, we haven't slept together. She seems reluctant to have sex. I'm not sure what's happening. But I think she cares for me."

"Son, a word of advice. Have sex with her first, before you declare your love. See if she's a good partner. Who is this girl?"

"I get this feeling she's had some bad experience she doesn't want to talk about. She works here as a showgirl. Her name's Suzanne Cane. You know, the one you checked on to see if she was married."

Sol paused before responding. "Yes, I remember now."

"We've been dating for a few weeks. Just on our nights off. One night I took her to the Library Club after work. But she doesn't like staying out late. That's funny for someone in a show."

Sol drained his martini glass, popped the olive in his mouth, and extinguished the cigar. "I don't think you've ever mentioned a woman before."

"I haven't had a girlfriend in the two years I've been here. Suzanne is special. You'll think so, too, when you meet her."

"When do I get to do that?" Sol asked.

"Soon, Unc. I'll invite you over for dinner in a week or so. Suzanne loves my cooking." Alan smiled and smacked his lips.

"I can see you're serious, cooking dinner for her. I'll look forward to it."

Alan finished his Scotch. "Gotta go, Unc. See you tomorrow night. You coming in?"

"Probably. Hardly a day goes by, I don't come to the casino. Can't seem to stay away." Sol's job was to be available for the dealers and Pit Bosses in cases of problems or grievances. But he loved the gambling industry and loved walking around the tables, watching the people. He liked watching life happen on their faces.

Alan headed toward the employees exit, and Sol took the elevator to the eleventh floor. He left the elevator and passed a large sign that read PERSONNEL OFFICES. He glanced at his watch. 3 a.m. Behind each office door, darkness. He headed down a long hallway and stopped at a door marked: ENTRANCE PROHIBITED WITHOUT AUTHORIZATION. He took a ring of keys from his pocket, opened the door, reached inside and flipped on the lights. Around the large room were file cabinets stacked nearly to the ceiling. He quickly found the C's, having been there before, opened the drawer, and removed Suzanne Cane's file.

He picked up a memo pad and printed in large, clear letters: RELIEVED OF VIP PARTIES. NOT ON CALL. He wrote in the date and signed it. Then he anchored it under a paper clip on the front page of Suzanne's file and returned the file to the drawer, locked the room, and headed into another office. ART CASSIO—Director of Personnel—was printed on the smoked-glass door. Sol took another pad from the desk and wrote: "*Suzanne Cane will be relieved of all VIP parties and after-hour duties as of 6/12/76.*" He signed his name and placed it in a prominent position on Art's desk. He let himself out; making sure the door was locked, and walked to the elevator. A security guard in blue uniform, complete with gun on his hip, came hustling around the corner.

"Oh. It's you, Mr. Wolfe. Sorry. We saw someone on camera in the personnel office. Thought I'd check it out."

"Good idea. Can't be too careful. Good work, son." Sol stepped into the open elevator and pushed the button for the lobby.

Wanda

Wanda stretched beneath the green silk sheets in Sol's huge bed, late morning light filtering through thick lashes. She heard him in the shower. Opening her eyes fully, she gazed around the room. His clothes were neatly hung in the open walk-in closet. A framed, paper-cut piece of art from China, with cranes flying over mountains, hung over his dresser. The opposite wall held a small Matisse. Her lavender evening dress lay in a heap on the yellow chair, purple panties bunched on top.

Examining her feelings for Sol was something she had avoided. Now, she had to admit to herself that she was falling in love. He was so good to her, kind, considerate, generous, and he had told her last night he loved her. But she wasn't ready to say the same words back to him. There had been too many relationships that ended in disappointment. She needed more time and had told him that. She did respect and admire him greatly. He was so confident and interested in every aspect of life. That attracted her. She heard the faucet shut off, and Sol shuffled into the bedroom with a towel wrapped around his waist.

"Good morning, sleepyhead. I have an appointment at one, so I need to get going." He leaned down and kissed her lingeringly. "Otherwise, I'd climb back into bed and cuddle my love."

She wrapped her arms around his neck and pulled him down. "If you didn't have an appointment, I'd expect more than a cuddle."

"Why am I not surprised, my insatiable woman?"

Sol stood and dropped his towel. His trim body hadn't changed since his thirties. Slipping into a blue shirt, he turned toward her, penis bowing its head, after some indecision.

Wanda loved watching him dress. He took diamond cuff links from the dresser and inserted them into wide shirt cuffs. He stepped into boxer shorts, donned navy slacks, and chose a blue linen jacket from the closet.

Walking back to the bed, he said, "Want me to pick you up tonight at the club?"

She nodded. "That would be nice." She took his hand and laid it on her cheek.

He kissed her again. "Be careful, lady. You'll spoil the line of my slacks."

Wanda laughed. "Have a good day."

"And you too, my love." Sol stood and picked up his keys. She heard him let himself out of the penthouse. The elevator returning to the lobby was the last sound of his departure.

She threw back the covers and headed for the bath. Turning on gold faucets, she adjusted the water to the right temperature. With a sprinkling of bubble bath particles, the foam swirled as the jets spurted on full force. Lowering her body into the warm water, she watched the froth build little snow cones on her stomach. On the marble floor, a stack of green Egyptian cotton towels rested beside the Jacuzzi. She could get used to this life of luxury and leisure. She just wanted to be sure this was what she wanted.

Wanda and Suzanne

*S*uzanne stretched lazily in her cozy double bed. Morning light filtered between ivory slats, casting white stripes across her blue bedspread. Last night she and Alan had stopped by the Library Club for a quick supper. She had left her car in the hotel parking lot, and Alan had driven her home. Hopefully she could get a ride with Wanda to rehearsals.

Her life had taken an exciting turn. She was seeing Alan Wolfe almost every free minute. She was never called anymore to entertain after the show. That in itself was wonderful. The only thing that worried her was that someone would discover she was being overlooked and start calling her again for the parties. She knew she should tell Alan why she wouldn't sleep with him, but she was scared. If he knew, he wouldn't want any part of her. Who would want a woman that slept with any high roller who paid for her body? She didn't even remember their names, and some she didn't ask. If she could only forget that part of her life all together. She heard Wanda in the kitchen making coffee. She picked up her watch and checked the time. Noon. She slipped out of bed into a blue robe, and walked barefoot to the kitchen.

"Morning." Suzanne poured a cup of fresh brew.

"Well, Miss Night Owl," Wanda said. "I got home at 4 a.m., and you weren't home. Where did you go after the show? You said you weren't being called for any late-night parties, so what's up with my roommate?" Wanda balanced on one leg, the other wrapped around her calf like an ostrich.

"I told you about Alan. He took me to the Library Club last night for dinner. We got to talking and forgot how late it was."

"So is this serious? Are you two in love?"

"I don't know, Wanda. I've been wanting to talk to you. You know I can't…haven't slept with him. He's so understanding. He hasn't pushed me at all. We start making out and then I just freeze up. I feel like I want to, but I'm afraid."

"What are you afraid of?" Wanda asked.

"I don't know. I feel really happy with him, I feel desire, and then something happens, and I get all tight and nervous. I was wondering if you have any suggestions."

"I know a good shrink. Maybe you should try that."

"I'm serious, Wanda. I want to make love to Alan, but I can't let myself go."

"I *am* serious. You need some help here. I don't know what is best for you, but certainly a shrink could find out and help."

"Maybe. I'll see." Suzanne spoke thoughtfully.

"Any other problems to ask Big Sister?" Wanda joked.

"Yes, are you going out this afternoon?"

"Yes, as a matter of fact, I'm going to a dance class."

"Could you drop me at the hotel between two and

three? I have a rehearsal. I'd be grateful. I left my car in the parking lot last night."

"No problem, but we have to hustle. You use the shower first."

"Okay." Suzanne hurried off to get ready.

Wanda sat at the kitchen table, drinking coffee and speculating on Suzanne's sexual hang-up. In a town where even important business deals were sometimes negotiated in a horizontal position, it could be a definite liability not to be able to fuck.

Ruby and Craig

*C*raig motioned Ruby to take a seat in the third row.

"Do we have to sit so close?" she whispered.

"Yes," he answered. With his arm firmly on hers, he guided her past a couple of men, and they took their seats in the middle.

Ruby was nervous. She had questioned Craig about tonight, but all he would say was, "You'll see."

She wore a pair of dark slacks and a dark blouse, at Craig's suggestion, not her usual wardrobe. She had found them at the back of her closet, something she had brought with her from Kentucky.

The room began to fill up, and then everyone fell silent. A man in his fifties took the podium. He was dressed in a suit and tie, and his shoes looked recently polished.

"Hi, welcome to the Westside Tuesday night group. I'm Dave, and I'm your chairperson tonight. I'm going to ask Ken to read from the *Big Book of Alcoholics Anonymous.*"

A young man in the front row stood, holding a large volume. "I'm Ken, and I'm a recovering alcoholic. I'd like to read from Chapter five, entitled, How It Works." The chapter dealt with accepting the simple program and following the path. When Ken had finished, another man was asked to read the twelve steps. Ruby heard, "One—We admit we are powerless over alcohol and our lives had become unmanageable. Two—We've come to believe that a power greater than ourselves could restore us to sanity..."

Ruby wanted to shrink and disappear. She wasn't like these people. Her gaze wandered around the room. On the wall above the chairperson, she read: EASY DOES IT and ONE DAY AT A TIME.

A tall man in the second row spoke. He had thinning gray hair and pale skin. His hands trembled slightly. A long-sleeved shirt and clean pressed slacks presented a good appearance.

"My name is John, and I'm a recovering alcoholic." His voice was thin but carried to the back rows because of the silence.

Ruby felt she didn't belong here. How dare Craig assume she did. She looked at him crossly, but he was staring straight ahead. She started to stand up, but Craig's large hand caught her on the forearm and pressed her back down. She guessed she'd just have to sit through this meeting, whether she liked it or not. The man continued speaking.

"I was married and had four kids to support. I had a good job in construction, and those of you in the building business know it's good pay and regular work. I used to stop at the bar with the boys after work. Gradually, I began drinking more and more and eventually didn't make it home at all. I lost my job, my wife, kids, and my house, and ended up a drunk on the streets. I stole from my best friend to buy booze. After ten years of bumming around in a drunken haze, I ended up in the hospital with pneumonia. My old friend that I stole from came to visit me, and when I got out, he brought me to AA. I have practiced the 12-step program and been sober for the last two years. Now I am an office manager for a construction company. I see my daughters twice a week. I feel good about myself for the first time in years. I am grateful for all that has been given to me, but I am most grateful for helping myself." John stopped speaking and sat down.

Ruby thought she would die of embarrassment. Were they all looking at her, thinking she was an alcoholic, too? Well, she wasn't. Craig took her hand in his and held it loosely.

She looked down at his work-worn hand, remembering her father's, the Reverend, his soft white pudgy ones holding her tightly against his naked belly. Tears rolled down her cheeks. Ruby's shoulders shook and she started to sob. Craig reached his arm round her shoulders and pulled her close. No one seemed to hear her as she ventured a look around. She continued to weep for the rest of the meeting. Wiping her nose and eyes, she finally gained control of her emotions. My God, she hadn't felt this relieved in years. Could a few tears do this?

At one point in the meeting, Dave Callahan asked if anyone was new to the meeting. Then he asked if anyone was new in sobriety? Ruby looked down at the floor, hoping no one would notice her.

"We're going to send around a basket for a dona-tion," Dave said. "This meeting has no funding other than your wallets. We thank you."

Then he announced that tea and cookies would be served. He invited everyone to stay.

"Want to stay for dessert?" Craig asked.

Ruby shook her head. "No, Craig, please. Let's just leave." She looked at him with such beseeching eyes that he stood and silently led the way out of the church.

Once on the street, Ruby turned to Craig. "Why didn't you tell me what that meeting was about?" She spoke accusingly, but much of initial anger at him had dissipated with her tears.

"I knew if I told you it was an AA meeting, you wouldn't come. I just wanted you to sit through one."

"You were very unfair! I don't intend to go to any more."

Craig looked down at her as they walked to his cab. "Ruby, you are a damn fine woman and could be even more than you are now, but you need help. I am a recovering alcoholic, and I got help."

Ruby stared up at him. "But you never drink, Craig. How come you still call yourself an alcoholic?"

He opened the door for her. "Because part of the 12-step program is that we always refer to ourselves as alcoholics. Any of us could go back with a single drink of liquor."

Ruby slid in the seat. She would have to think about this. She certainly did feel better.

Except that she wanted a drink as soon as she got home. But she didn't dare ask Craig to stop at a liquor store. Perhaps she could get Suzanne to buy her a bottle. Damn. If she could only find that bottle she stashed.

Craig drove her home and parked in front of the apartment building.

She looked at him. "Wanna' come up?" She smiled and turned her best come-hither look on him.

He took her hand in both of his and held her gaze. "Ruby. I want you for my woman. But not the way you are now. I want you sober. But you have to want it, too. It doesn't work unless you want to get sober. I think I'll wait on our sex life a while. I care about you and I hope that you will come to care for me. I'm not very good at saying these things. Hope I've made myself clear."

Ruby was surprised. She had never had a man declare that much of an interest. And she was surprised and a little disappointed that he wouldn't come up. She nodded and opened her door. She started to deny that she needed to get sober, as Craig put it, but changed her mind. She leaned down and spoke through the open window. "When will I see you again?"

"I'll call tomorrow, my day off. Wanna' go on a picnic? Maybe out to Lake Mead?"

Ruby nodded again. She hadn't gone on a picnic in her entire adult life. She couldn't remember her last real date. "Sure."

"I'll call in the morning. And Ruby, please don't drink tonight. It means a lot to me. And it will to you too before long."

"Okay," Ruby spoke tentatively. She had hoped to have a few just to steady her nerves before bed. But there wasn't any liquor in the apartment. None she could find.

"I'll try."

When she looked back, Craig's cab was sailing down Karen Drive. Her roommate, Violet, was not home yet. Her car was not in the carport, and Ruby desperately wanted a drink.

Alan and Suzanne — Sol and Wanda

$\mathcal{A}$lan heard the doorbell as he opened the bottle of wine. Suzanne was in the dining room, admiring the table.

He greeted his uncle and Wanda. "Welcome to the Wolfe's den restaurant," he said, showing them into the living room.

Everyone grinned at Alan's little joke.

Suzanne smoothed her blue linen sheath, took a deep breath, and turned toward Alan's uncle.

"Uncle Sol, this is Suzanne." Alan slid his arm around her waist.

Sol offered his hand. "It's a pleasure, my dear."

She smiled, placing her hand in his, feeling a small flutter inside. She was thinking of him reading her personnel file. "I've heard so much about you, sir."

"I hope most of it was good."

"Oh, it was." She looked at Alan.

Sol turned to Wanda. "I believe you and my nephew know each other."

"Oh yes. Alan has been to our apartment a few times," Wanda said.

When Alan had first told Sol that Suzanne's roommate was Wanda Moon, Sol had been pleasantly surprised. Now he replied, "Who would have thought the most important ladies in our lives would be roommates?"

Boots, the large Persian cat headed straight for Suzanne, folding his tail around her ankle.

She reached down, stroking his softness. "Hello, you darling cat."

"I think Suzanne likes Boots better than me," Alan said, and grinned. "Please. Have a seat. What would the ladies like to quench their thirst?"

"I'll have a glass of wine," Wanda said, choosing to settle in the leather chair.

"I'll have the same," Suzanne said as she sat on the couch.

"Alan, may I pour the wine?" Sol asked.

"Sure thing, Unc." Alan took Wanda's silk shawl and Sol's cream linen jacket and disappeared into the bedroom.

In the kitchen, a bottle of French wine stood on the counter, breathing. Alan returned and took the coq au vin from the oven.

"Wow, I think I've been missing something here, son. I didn't realize you were such a good cook." Sol often referred to his nephew as his son, since he had no children of his own. And indeed, he often wished Alan were his son.

Sol poured two glasses of wine and headed for the living room. Alan followed, went behind the bar and poured Scotch for himself and Sol.

Sol offered a toast. "Long live beautiful women."

Alan lifted his glass. "I'll drink to that."

After the toast, Wanda complimented the wine. "This is very nice, Alan. What is it?"

"Cote de Rhone, 1970," Alan replied. "It's five years old."

"It's certainly delicious," Suzanne agreed.

Alan turned to Wanda. "What do you think of my uncle's pad?"

"It's a wonderful place," Wanda said, as she sipped her wine.

"Uncle Sol has a penthouse overlooking the Strip," Alan explained to Suzanne. "Original paintings on the walls, very plush."

Suzanne nodded. "I've heard about the paintings from Wanda, and the view."

"We can't all live in penthouses like my uncle, but if you will be seated at my humble table, dinner is served." Alan led the way to the dining room.

Sol pulled out chairs for the women. Pink carnations in a low bowl adorned the middle of the table. Each place setting had a blue napkin beside the silverware. The placemats were blue and purple striped. Sol was impressed. He knew his nephew hadn't bothered with these things before Suzanne came into his life.

The chicken dish was delicious as was the chilled asparagus, and the Caesar salad which had become Alan's specialty, was crisp and fresh.

When everyone was served, Sol asked Suzanne, "Do you like your job at the El Morocco?"

Suzanne was startled but recovered quickly. "Uh… yes, I do. I like performing, and I like the money."

Sol glanced across the table at his nephew. "If you ever get tired of being a showgirl we can find you a position at a desk upstairs in the offices, and the pay would be the same as you are getting now."

Suzanne was surprised. "I appreciate that offer, Mr. Wolfe. I don't anticipate not wanting to perform, but if I do, I'll let you know."

"That was mighty nice of you, Unc." Turning to Suzanne, he explained, "My uncle can hire and fire as he pleases."

Sol nodded. "No need to call me Mr. Wolfe. Sol is fine."

Suzanne smiled and was feeling more relaxed. "Thanks, Sol."

The apple pie that Alan had made was mouthwatering. The girls and the men ate large pieces.

"You'll make some girl a fine husband, Alan," his uncle said, grinning.

Sol and Wanda said their goodnights early because Wanda had a morning dance class. When the door closed, Suzanne was standing in front of Alan. He slipped his arms around her waist and turned her around. His lips claimed her mouth with all the hunger he'd been holding back. His erection against her thigh, his hands moved down her back, cupping her cheeks. He gradually moved one hand between their bodies, fingers reaching beneath her panties. She was breathing in short gasps

"Oh, Alan," she murmured.

He scooped her up, and carried her to the bedroom, gently placing her on the green chenille spread. After he slipped off her bikini panties, his fingers found her most sensitive spot. He was afraid to take his hand away to undress himself for fear she would change her mind. But in a swift movement, he removed his slacks. She had her arms around his shoulders and began tugging at his shirt. He bit the lobe of her ear, nibbling gently along her neck, trailing his tongue over her breasts, and down the soft curve of her belly. When he finally settled down with his chin between her thighs, Suzanne was ready. Small murmurs escaped her lips. Her hips arched, she ached for more, her moans growing stronger. When he finally brought her to climax, she uttered a low, animal sound. He immediately entered her and, pacing himself, brought her again to orgasm as his own burst upon him.

She clutched him tightly to her breasts, whispering in his ear. "That was incredible. I've never experienced anything like that before."

Alan lifted his head from her shoulder. "I love you, Suzanne."

She wanted to tell him she thought she loved him, too. But remembering her secret, she felt the old fear return. Her body stiffened, and Alan could sense her pulling away.

"What's wrong, honey? Tell me. I want to know. Whatever it is, I can help."

She shook her head and began to cry. "I can't tell you. You wouldn't love me anymore."

"There is nothing you can tell me to change my feelings."

Please, let it go for now."

Alan knew when to retreat. "Okay. But remember, I want to help you." He held her for a long time. They began kissing again. She returned his passion, and they made love to each other long into the night until they fell asleep in each other's arms.

Wanda Moon

Wanda lay still on an Indian blanket, the red bikini beckoning the morning sun to anoint her brown body. A chartreuse gecko climbed her leg and crawled to the center of her stomach. Thin red eyes peered into hers. She felt transparent, full of light. Memories of ancestral spirits hummed in her ears like the forest music at first dawn. The gift surfaced. Her mind quieted. A familiar voice rose above the droning.

"My little moon, you are far from your people. Your brother is treading the path of danger. Your sisters are helpless. I am no longer in my earthly body. I have gone to the great beyond, to join your mother. You are needed by your family."

The voice of her father spilled over her like white-water rapids, swift and unrelenting. She saw him, long gray hair flowing around his shoulders. He carried a staff with a deer horn handle, passed down through generations in her tribe. Her body stiffened, as in orgasm. Her legs shuddered in a fit of tremors, then softly relaxed.

"Hieeeee," sprang from her throat. The gift had not come to her for a very long time. Not since she had left the reservation. Something was wrong with her brother, Brady. Black Bear, her father, had spoken.

Wanda sat up with a start, brushing hair from her eyes. Gasping for breath, she saw her disheveled bed, covers on the floor. She had been dreaming! However, that made it no less of an event. She knew that her ancestors often appeared when the mind was at rest. My God! Her father was gone! And Brady was in trouble. She felt sad that no one had let her know her father had died. Of course, how could they? She had not contacted her family since she ran away.

Barefoot, she padded to the kitchen and put on a pot of coffee. Back down the hall, she peeked into Suzanne's room. She was still asleep, blond locks flowing over white sheets. Wanda headed for the shower. While warm jets of water massaged her body, she contemplated what she must do. She would have to call her oldest sister, Naomi, and find out what exactly was happening with Brady. She hated giving up her anonymity, and she dreaded hearing Naomi's disapproval. But she had no choice. She could not ignore her father's visitation. Guilt flowed over her, an unwanted visitor. Abandoning one's family was bad enough, but she hadn't been there when her father passed to the other world.

"Damn," she uttered against the stream of water in her mouth.

⌐

Dressed in red slacks and a red tank top, Wanda picked up the phone, giving the operator the long, unused number.

After three rings she heard Naomi's deep voice, "Hullo."

Wanda hesitated, "Naomi. It's Wanda."

A long silence on the line across the miles. "Wanda? Where are you?"

Wanda ignored the question. "I'm calling about Brady. I...I had a feeling he's in trouble. What's happening?"

"He's in jail. White man's jail. Caught selling marijuana off the reservation. Bail is too high for us. His case comes up in a couple of weeks."

"I'll try to come down."

Her sister was silent.

"How is the rest of the family? Is Iris okay?" Iris was Wanda's younger sister.

"Black Bear, our father, is dead," she told Wanda.

"Yes, I know. How is Iris?" Wanda repeated.

"She married Big Bill, just before Blackie died. She's fine, expecting her first."

Big Bill was the old chief's son. So her father had finally tied the two families together. He had wanted Wanda to marry Big Bill.

"How did you know Blackie was dead?" Naomi asked.

"The gift visited me. That's why I'm calling."

Naomi repeated her question. "Where are you?"

"I don't want to say right now. I'll explain when I come down."

"Sure." Naomi didn't sound convinced.

"I'll be in touch, goodbye for now." Wanda's hand trembled as she replaced the phone. She felt even more remote from Naomi than she had growing up. Their mother had died when Wanda was eight and Naomi was twelve. Naomi had tried to become a mother to her two sisters and Brady. It had worked with Iris and

Brady but not Wanda. She was the rebel that Naomi could never control.

Could Wanda convince Richie, her boss at the club, that she needed a few days off for family emergency? She didn't remember him ever giving anyone time off, for any reason. She felt a lump forming in the middle of her chest. She grabbed her practice clothes and her keys and headed out the door. Better to work out this dilemma in dance class.

Sol

*M*arina, Sol's housekeeper, served scrambled eggs and bacon, toast and coffee to Sol and Wanda at the table overlooking the city. In the distance, Mount Charleston stood against the blue Nevada sky, dancing behind the shimmering waves of heat emanating from the flat, pale land.

Sol was reading the racing form. "I have a meeting at The Sands this afternoon. Do you want me to drop you at your apartment?"

"No, I'll take a cab." Wanda wanted to discuss her brother's trouble with Sol but wasn't sure this was the time. "Are you in a hurry?"

"No, honey, I got time. What's up?"

Wanda took a deep breath. She told him quickly about her brother being in jail, her phone call to Naomi after seven years of silence.

"How did you know Brady was in jail?" he asked.

Wanda looked directly at him. "I had a dream. My father visited me from beyond. He told me that I was needed by the family."

Sol nodded, showing no surprise. He folded the paper and put it aside. "So what will you do?"

"I need to go down for Brady's' hearing in court. I don't have enough money for bail, but I can give him moral support. Perhaps I can hire a lawyer down there. I have a little money saved. I'm not sure, Sol. I just know I have to go. My father told me to go. But I don't think Richie will give me any time off. And I can't lose my job at the club. If I just go, Richie may not take me back." Having summed up her situation, she felt a small relief.

Sol was silent, thinking. Finally, he put his hand over hers. "If you need money, I have it. I will give you as much as you need to help your family. As far as Richie goes, why worry about it until you talk to him? Let's take one thing at a time."

Wanda wasn't sure she could take money from Sol. "I don't know. I don't want to be indebted to you."

"Sweetheart, I have more than I can ever spend. Let me help you with your family. Consider it a gift. A repayment of all the happiness you've given me." He hesitated. "Would you let me come with you when your brother has his hearing? We could have a lawyer in place by then."

Wanda laughed. "I'm not sure you would be at ease in my family's humble surroundings. I'm hardly at ease myself. There are no luxuries on the reservation." She wondered if he would still love her after he saw the squalor of her family. She leaned over and kissed him on the mouth. "I'll think about your offer. Thank you. You are a sweet and generous man."

Sol stood. "I do have to go now, love." He laid two twenties on the table for her cab fare, grabbed his Italian silk jacket and headed for the door. "Pick you up tonight after your last show."

He headed for the garage and his Rolls. Backing out, he dialed a number on his car phone.

"Hullo." Richie Abrams hoarse voice came over the line.

"Sol here. How the hell are you, Richie?"

"Sol. Christ. Haven't heard from you in months. What's goin' on?"

"I need a favor, Richie. I'll make it worth your while. One of your strippers, Angel Moon, has a family emergency. She needs a few days to a week to go down to Arizona. I want you to let her have a leave of absence."

"Christ, Sol. If I give her leave, I'll have to do it for all the broads. I'd never be able to count on them being here anymore."

"I don't have the answer to that problem, but this is really important to me, Richie."

"So is Angel your new woman?"

"Yes."

Richie said no more.

"Okay, Sol. You got your favor. You owe me one now."

"Absolutely. And Richie, when she asks for time off, don't tell her about our conversation."

"Understood, Sol. How come I never see you at the gym, anymore?"

"I'm getting my gymnastics in bed these days."

Richie roared. "I should be so lucky."

"Thanks, pal. I won't forget. See ya' around."

Sol made another call to his bookmaker as he drove into the Sands valet parking. He placed a bet on the

L.A. Lakers, and on Island Sun to win in the fifth at Pimlico. He tipped the valet a fifty, and cautioning him about the Rolls, then entered the hotel.

The lobby was filled with tourists. About thirty people were lined up at the front desk. Tourism, as always, was a big draw for this town. People from all over the U.S. and Europe visited Las Vegas. The twenty-four-hour casinos, restaurants, clubs and theaters were the reason it was called "the town that never sleeps." Even some residents had a hard time falling asleep after their shift was over.

Las Vegas was a shimmering mirage of entertainment, vice, anger, and crime. A lot of anger was generated from the have-nots to the haves. Crime was higher on the north side, but nonviolent crimes were prevalent on the south side on the Strip. Pickpockets, ladies of the night and day, drug dealers, casino managers, Pit Bosses, all who attempted to rip off their customers or bosses; Las Vegas was a wide-open town.

Sol headed for the nightclub off the lobby. On his right he saw Stony "The Ace" Brooks, a representative for some of the owners back East.

"Hi, Sol. How are you?" They shook hands and entered the club.

"Pretty good. How about you?"

"Can't complain." Ace twisted his cuff link, a nervous habit. His pale, pockmarked face and gray crew cut revealed he was not a Vegas sun worshiper.

The club was closed this time of day, thus making it perfect for a meeting. Several men took seats around a long table covered with a white cloth. A waiter poured Borolo into crystal glasses. Later, lunch would be served. Usually, it was Ziti with meat sauce, Sicilian spaghetti. Sol didn't look forward to the business at hand. What to do with a small downtown casino that was being skimmed by the management.

Violet and Nick

*T*hey left the Calendar Club and drove to the Village Pub on Flamingo Boulevard. Nick was meeting someone before they went to his place for the night. They walked to a back booth and sat down next to each other. The waitress took their order. Nick's was Beefeaters on the rocks and Violet's was a dry martini.

After their drinks arrived, a middle-aged man with a pale pockmarked face and a brown fedora, slid in the other side.

"Hi, Nick." He nodded toward Violet. "Do ya' think that was wise? Bringin' her here?"

"It's okay. She's an employee and my girl."

'I know that," the man replied, twisting his cuff link.

She recognized this man as one of the twelve she'd served in Nick's office several weeks ago.

"What's up?" Nick asked. "Why am I meeting you here tonight?"

"You got until next week to come up with a name." The man lit an unfiltered Lucky Strike, spitting tobacco particles on the floor.

"Okay. I think I know who it is."

"Yeah? Wanna' tell me now?"

"No, not yet. I don't want to get anyone in trouble until I'm absolutely sure."

"Next week, Nick." He slid from the booth and walked out the front door.

Violet looked down at her green olive in the bottom of her glass. She squeezed Nick's hand under the table. "Do you know who?" she asked, not looking at him.

"Maybe. I'm not sure."

"What did he mean that you had until next week?" She turned her beautiful purple eyes on him.

"He means if I don't come up with who is stealing from the casino, they will hold me responsible."

"How will they hold you responsible?"

He could feel Violet's pulses quicken as he held her wrist. "I'll probably lose my job and won't be able to get another in this town," Nick lied, as he ran fingers through his dark hair.

"Is that all that will happen, Nick?"

"I don't know, sweetheart. Don't worry. I'll come up with a name by next week."

They left the bar and walked to the corner where Nick was parked. Down the street at the end of the cul-de-sac was a topless club, Guys and Dolls. Violet had worked there briefly as a dancer/waitress when she had first come to town. In front of the club, standing next to the owner Gus, was the man they had just met in the bar. The two of them were smoking and talking. Violet kept her head turned as she climbed in the front seat. For some unknown reason, she did not want Gus to see her. She sensed she was enmeshed in a web so tenacious that even if she struggled, she could not free herself.

Alan

Alan put his coffee cup in the sink and went looking for Lou. Ten minutes had passed since she went to the bathroom. He found her naked, spread-eagled on the green chenille bedspread.

"I was wondering when you were gonna' come lookin' for me." She gave him a sexy smile.

"No, Lou. Get up and get dressed. No more trade. Just cash, and then you have to go. You do want your crank, don't you?" Alan shooed Boots off the bed because he seemed interested in what was between Lou's bare thighs. She flashed him a sullen frown and quickly dressed.

She followed Alan to the living room and dumped her purse on the leather couch to find a lone twenty-dollar bill. She handed it to him. In return, he gave her a tiny amount of white powder in a match box. If she was lucky, she would get four lines.

"What's happenin'? You got a girlfriend?" She tucked the box in her pocket and stuffed everything back into her bag.

"As a matter of fact, yes. Listen, you can't come here anymore. It's getting too dangerous. From now on, call me and I'll meet you."

"Don't want me to run into her, huh? Well, don't worry. I won't tell her you screwed me." Lou sniffed and rubbed her nose with the back of her hand.

"I wouldn't think you would tell her," Alan replied. "Otherwise, you might find it hard to buy crank in this town."

"Yeah, okay." Lou scowled, then a brighter thought entered her head. "Wanna' give me a line before I go for old times' sake?"

"No, Lou. And remember, no more dropping in."

He watched her back out of the drive. She was a habit he had vowed to stop. But he was concerned that his other customers might drop by when Suzanne was there. He'd instruct them all to call from now on. It was last week he first realized he was attracting attention. His neighbor, Benny, asked jokingly if he was book-making. Alan brushed it off saying he and his friends partied a lot. But he feared his excuse didn't ring true. He knew it was time to stop the traffic. From now on he would sell the speed he made away from his home.

He walked into the living room and sprinkled three lines of meth on the mirror. Snorting it through his raw nostrils, he savored the burning of his nasal passages and the kick-ass rush to his head.

Ruby

*R*uby put her purse and lunch in the locker and took out a sewing kit. She was working now at the Silver Slipper as a seamstress. Violet had heard they were hiring seamstresses for the revue, *Boylesque*, so she took Ruby for the interview, and when an example of her work was seen, she was hired on the spot.

She was an excellent seamstress, and the boys/girls in the revue showed their appreciation. "Ruby, could you stitch up this rip under my arm?" One of the guys hollered. "Guess my muscles are showing in all the wrong places. Thanks, sweetie, you're a doll."

Another performer grabbed Ruby's arm. "Hey, girl, help! The Velcro just failed in my crotch. Can't have my twins hanging out during the show now, can I?"

She would fix each performer's apparel with speed and care. Her hands would shake periodically when she sewed something intricate, but for the most part, she could perform her duties backstage as well as the guys did onstage.

The boys in the show were female impersonators and did a great job of impersonating Marilyn, Marlene, and Judy, among other famous personalities. Backstage was chaotic most every night, and Ruby usually helped the performers get their shit together as well as their costumes. She loved being needed. And she was definitely needed here.

"Hey, Ruby. Can you help me with this damn dress? It's caught on my wig!" Bentley waved his arms wildly.

Ruby dutifully pulled the feathered costume over his large head and smoothed it out over his buttocks.

"Thanks, hon. Now don't be getting fresh with me. Like those buns, huh? Real tight. Next time I find a dreamboat that goes both ways, I'll give you a turn. Does my hair stick up in back, sweetie?" After getting Ruby's assurance that he looked terrific, he pranced off to the kitchen for a quick nip. The guys always kept booze in the freezer, and at first Ruby was tempted, but she resisted.

Recently, one of the guys left a bottle of Scotch on the counter, and Ruby picked it up to put back in the freezer. She hesitated, remembering how nice the liquid felt sliding down her throat. Magically, it could blot out all the problems of her life. But she didn't have those problems anymore. She felt good about what she was doing. She'd fallen off the wagon a couple of times, but Craig had been there for her. Ruby opened the freezer and stuck the bottle on a shelf. She'd get to tell about this at the AA meeting next Monday.

Craig usually picked her up after the last show. Tonight, he was waiting in his cab when she came out the back of the club. He leaned across, opening the door.

She slid in and kissed him on the cheek.

"How'd it go tonight, honey?" He said, leaving the Slipper parking lot.

"Good. I had a few emergency stitches, but everything worked out fine."

"Think you kind of like working with those guys, don't cha?"

"I do. I really like the 'girls' in the show, as the boss calls them. They are for the most part very sweet and kind men. Of course, when things aren't going well, they can become bitchy queens. Worse than any woman I've ever worked with, and I've see a lot of backstage drama queens in my time."

That made Craig laugh. "Bet you have. Do you miss performing, honey?"

She thought a moment. "No, not anymore. I remember all the stress involved with being on stage. And getting ready to go on. I much prefer backstage. It's fun, and I feel like I'm doing something worthwhile."

Craig pulled into the carport at the apartment. He came around and opened Ruby's door.

She looked surprised. "You coming up? Don't you have to finish your shift?"

"Nope. I told the dispatcher I was takin' off the rest of the night. It's a special occasion."

"And what would that be, Craig?" She looked up into his strong face.

"Why, I'm gonna' make love to my woman. Nothin' more important than that." He pulled her close and kissed her, their bodies leaning against the cab.

Her arms encircled his neck, and she returned the kiss. Craig locked the cab with one hand, the other one around Ruby's waist.

"Come in to my parlor, my dear." Her voice was husky as she led him up the steps to her apartment.

Sol and Nick

$\mathcal{A}$ voluptuous blond was going through her motions on the Calendar Club stage. She'd just stripped to her G-string when Sol bet $2000 red at the roulette table.

"Seventeen black wins," the croupier called.

Several people groaned.

Sol's money was raked into the bank. He picked up his remaining chips and Scotch and left the table. He went to the cage and cashed in the $5000. He'd started with $2000. Not bad for fifteen minutes. Sol had learned long ago that the odds were always stacked in favor of the house. The very first time you lose, you withdraw. The only way to gamble. He slipped the bundle of money into his inside pocket, and stopped a beautiful waitress with violet-blue eyes.

"I'm looking for Nick Capela."

She hesitated, looking toward the bar. "Ask Eddie, the bartender. He'll know if he's in."

Placing a folded fifty on the inside ledge of the bar, Sol got Eddie's attention.

"I'd like to speak with Nick. My name is Sol Wolfe. I'm a stockholder in the casino."

Eddie deftly slipped the bill into his pocket. "I'll check and see if he's in, Mr. Wolfe. Have a seat. Want a fresh drink?"

Sol thanked him and shook his head.

Eddie picked up the house phone and cupped the

receiver with his hand. As soon as he hung up, the same waitress appeared at the bar. "Violet, show this gentleman to Nick's office."

Sol followed her down the hall. She knocked twice on a door with no knob. It sprung open immediately.

"Go right in, sir," Violet said.

Sol entered and saw a handsome man with dark wavy hair standing behind his desk.

"Good evening. I'm Nick Capela," the man said. He offered his hand.

"Sol Wolfe." They shook hands and without waiting for an invitation, Sol sat in the leather chair across from Nick.

Nick returned to his seat. "Don't think we've met before. You say you're a stockholder? You haven't' attended any of the meetings."

"That's true." Sol pulled a Havana from his breast pocket. "Like one?"

Nick shook his head.

Sol continued. "Usually Ace Brooks attends, so I don't feel I have to."

"You a friend of Ace's?" Nick asked uneasily.

Sol took his time lighting the end of the cigar with a gold lighter, sucking in air until it caught. "We're acquaintances."

"What did you want to see me about, Mr. Wolfe?"

"I strongly encourage you to make good the losses in this casino. Beg, borrow, whatever you need to do to pay back the stockholders." Sol stared at Nick.

"With all due respect, Mr. Wolfe, I don't have any assets. I cannot imagine who would lend me $100,000."

Sol puffed on his cigar. "I'd be willing to finance some of it."

Nick looked surprised. "Why would you do that?"

"I'd like to help if I can. I'd borrow small amounts from several different sources, if I were you. You know what will happen if you don't pay it back?"

Nick looked away, but his heart missed a beat. "I've discovered the guilty party. It seems to me that person must make up the losses."

Sol took the cigar from his mouth and slowly ground out the end on the arm of the brown leather chair. "I don't think you're hearing me, Nick. As manager, you are the responsibility party. One last time," Sol's voice grew louder, "Pay back the losses." Sol dropped the cigar to the carpet. He stood and walked to the door. He turned toward Nick and their eyes met. "I'd be very worried about my safety right now, if I were in your shoes."

He left the casino by the same door he came in. Climbing behind the wheel of his Rolls, he knew he had done all that he could to save Nick Capela. The greedy little asshole had just blown his last chance.

Wanda, Suzanne, Ruby and Violet

Wanda pulled into the Desert Winds Apartments and found a visitor parking space for her Carmen Ghia. She and Suzanne found Apartment 101 and knocked.

A dark-haired girl with purple eyes opened the door. The aroma of freshly perked coffee drifted from the kitchen.

"Hi. I'm Wanda Moon. I'm here to see Ruby. This is my roommate, Suzanne."

"Come in, please. I'm Violet, Ruby's roommate. Ruby," Violet called, "Wanda Moon is here."

Ruby came down the hall, cigarette in hand. "It's been a long time, Wanda."

"Sure has. Good to see you again." Wanda introduced Suzanne to Ruby, and they exchanged greetings.

"Have a seat." Violet motioned to the couch.

Wanda turned to Ruby, "You said on the phone you were doing costumes at the Slipper, but you wanted extra work."

Ruby nodded.

"I need a couple of new costumes, and I thought perhaps you could design and make them."

"Sure, I can make anything."

"I want a feathered Carmen Miranda-type costume and a large hat with fruit on top. How does that sound? "

"Sound like fun," Ruby said. "Yeah, I can do that."

"Then I want a Vampira look…all black with a long

cape." Wanda brought forth a piece of paper with two sketches on it. "Of course, include the G-string with Velcro on both costumes."

Ruby looked at the sketches. "Sure, when do you need them finished?"

"Oh, three or four weeks, no deadline. I haven't found the music yet or worked up a routine. What do you charge an hour?"

"Ruby works for $50 an hour, plus materials," Violet jumped in.

Ruby looked from Violet to Wanda and nodded.

Wanda smiled. "Fine. That sounds fair to me. So let me know when you get the fabrics so I can see them before you start sewing."

"Okay," Ruby said, smiling, too.

"I just made a pot of coffee. Anyone like a cup?" Violet said on her way to the kitchen.

"Sounds good," Suzanne said.

"Me, too," Wanda added. "How do you like working at the Silver Slipper, Ruby?"

"I really like it. It's a lot of fun. Never a dull moment with the boys in the show."

"I can imagine," Wanda said. "By the way, keep my costumes out of the sight of the boys. I'll bet at least on of them would love to dress up in them."

The girls laughed. "No chance of that," Ruby said. "I do my extra sewing at home."

Violet returned with a trayful of cups, coffee pot and cream and sugar. The four women drank coffee, smoked Marlboros, and traded show gossip. Then they started on the men in their lives.

Ruby told them about Craig. "He's so good to me. He and Violet are responsible for my being sober." She cast a grateful look at her roommate.

"No, Ruby, you did it yourself. You had the strength and desire to do it. Craig and I are very proud of you."

"I admire you too, Ruby," Wanda said. "It's not easy to resist temptation in this town."

Ruby beamed. "I've even quit the sleeping pills at night and the bennies in the morning."

"That's pretty impressive. I still take a sleeping pill to go to sleep," Wanda admitted. "Most of this town couldn't get by without their pills."

"Ain't that a fact," Violet said, and they all laughed again.

Ruby laid down the sketches and started scratching her arms.

"Did you get poison oak or bitten by an insect?" Wanda asked.

A look of embarrassment crossed Ruby's face. "No. It's a reaction to my withdrawal."

"How long does it continue?" Wanda asked.

"It depends," Ruby said. "The guys at AA say it could go for a few months. But I don't mind. I'm feeling so much better than I have in such a long time."

"Ruby, if you come by my apartment, I have some ointment for that. It's an old Indian remedy." She grinned.

"You mean it, Wanda? I'd love to have something to speed up the recovery."

Wanda wrote down the address and phone number and handed it to Ruby. "Call me when you want to come to make sure I'm home. Midafternoon is a good time."

"What about you, Violet?" Suzanne asked. "Any particular man in your life?"

Violet looked serious. "I'm seeing my boss, but he's married, so I don't broadcast it. His wife is in a sanitarium."

Wanda nodded. "What's his name?"

"Nick Capela. Please don't say anything to anyone."

"Not to worry. Suzanne and I will tell no one."

Violet looked so forlorn that Wanda asked, "Is anything wrong?"

Violet knew she could not talk about Nick's trouble to anyone. "No," she said.

"If I can help you in anyway, let me know." Wanda squeezed Violet's arm. Then she turned to Ruby. "Would you like me to spread the word at the Club that you're available for making costumes?"

"That would be great. Thank you, Wanda."

"Okay. Suzanne and I are off to dance class. Talk to you girls later. I'm so glad you're well, Ruby. Nice meeting you, Violet."

Violet smiled but wouldn't meet Wanda's eyes.

The girls waved as Suzanne and Wanda left.

In the car, Wanda said, "It's really good to know

Ruby is turning her life around. She has a supportive roommate, too. That helps."

"It certainly does." Suzanne squeezed Wanda's arm.

Wanda and Sol

*T*hey had just made the Needles turnoff from Interstate 40 and were on the last sixty miles. Wanda's family lived on the Colorado River Indian Reservation outside of Parker, Arizona. Sol was at the wheel of the rented Cadillac Eldorado, Wanda by his side, and Irving, Sol's attorney, in the backseat. Wanda had convinced Sol not to drive the Rolls down. She was sure the Indian children would scratch it climbing all over the car.

Wanda had accepted Sol's offer to pay for Brady's lawyer and bail. She knew in her heart that he genuinely wanted to help. However, she was surprised when Richie had agreed to her request for a few days off.

"I've been thinking about a family emergency leave for my employees," he said, "and this seems like a good time to start. But if anyone abuses it, then it will be no time off at all, like before."

She had thanked him and told him she'd return within three or four days. "I'll let you know when we leave," she said.

Again he surprised her with, "Don't hurry back, doll, if you think your family needs you."

For a minute she was scared. "You aren't going to fire me, are you, Richie?"

"Hell no, of course not. You're too good for the house. I'll just make the other girls work harder while you're gone." He smiled wickedly and patted her on the shoulder and wished her luck with her brother's hearing. Wanda couldn't remember him ever showing any interest in anyone's personal business. And he'd never patted her on the shoulder before.

When Wanda told Roxy that Richie assured her she would still have her job, Roxy said, "Of course, babe, he damn well knows if he fired you, I'd never fuck him again."

She stopped remembering and studied the landscape. Large hills of rock and a long plateau of cracked earth reached to the blue-gray mountains in the distance. The Cadillac smoothly sped by high desert Cholla trees along the two-lane black top. Cactus, yucca trees and scrub brush dotted the parched land.

Wanda glanced in back. Irv, as Sol called him, was snoring. Locks of thinning gray hair fluffed around his ears. His ruddy complexion stood out against the gray upholstery. He would represent Brady in the hearing tomorrow. Irving Samuels had been Sol's attorney for twenty years and had seen him through many unusual circumstances.

"I need you to do whatever you must to get this kid off or the lightest sentence possible," Sol had instructed Irv before they left.

Irv knew money was no problem. And he knew money could arrange things in Brady's favor. Fortunately, he had a license to practice in Arizona, as well as Nevada and California.

Sol lit a cigarette and cracked the window. A blast of hot air like a jet taking off hit his cheek in spite of the air-conditioner. "Christ, it's hot here. Must be hotter than Vegas."

Wanda laughed. "It's a drier heat than Vegas. The Mohave Triangle is supposed to be one of the hottest places in North America. It covers Death Valley to Needles, south to Blythe, north to Parker."

When they finally turned right onto the bridge at Earp, the Colorado River, azure-blue and inviting, flowed beneath them. Several recreational boats and jet skis skimmed over the glistening waters.

Ten minutes later, Wanda pointed out the lane to her sister Naomi's house. Driving down a dirt road, with melons and corn growing on either side, they came to a faded pink stucco building. Several rusted cars were scattered around the yard. Clothes hung on a line on a windless day, bleached white in the afternoon sun. Three baskets of corn in their husks stood on the front porch. The third step up was missing.

Wanda's cheeks burned. She was ashamed of her family. Indian trash was what the white children used to call her when she was a child. She glanced at Sol. The gray Cadillac came to an abrupt stop. He looked over at Wanda and smiled, covering her hand.

"Hey, lady, I love you."

A taller, older version of Wanda stepped out on the porch. Her large black eyes took everything in. She had been a beauty once. She wore a faded housedress that hung loosely on her frame. In place of the jet-black hair Wanda remembered, two graying braids fell to her waist. Long turquoise earrings dangled from her ears as she hopped over the missing step.

They all climbed from the car, stretching their cramped limbs.

Naomi held out her hands, and Wanda took them. No hugs or embraces.

"Hello, Naomi." Wanda searched her sister's eyes for some affection but found only distance. "This is Sol Wolfe, my dear friend, and his attorney, Irving Samuels. My sister, Naomi Lightsmith."

Sol and Irv shook hands with Naomi. "It's a pleasure," Sol said.

"Likewise," Irv said.

Naomi eyed Irv's beige silk suit and Sol's white linen jacket. "You'll get them dirty real soon down here."

For a moment no one spoke. Wanda, one beat away from a nervous giggle, said, "Where's Jackson?" referring to Naomi's husband.

"He went into town. He'll be back soon. Come on in." She led them into her home. The interior was spotlessly clean and smelled of lavender and thyme. Above the windows, several bunches of herbs were tied upside down, drying.

"Have a seat." She motioned to Sol and Irv. They both removed their jackets and sat on the couch covered by a faded turquoise and yellow Indian blanket. Springs squeaked under their combined weights.

"Have you seen Brady today?" Wanda asked.

"Not today. I went to the jail yesterday, took him

some Indian fry bread and beans." Naomi sat across from the men, and Wanda sat next to her.

'How's he doing?"

"He's doing all right. Brady don't get riled up too easy. Guess maybe you've been away so long you don't remember."

Wanda ignored her sister's comment. "Irv is going to represent Brady tomorrow at the hearing. Do you know exactly what he's charged with?"

"Selling marijuana. Apparently, he sold a lid to an undercover cop from Phoenix. The sheriff thinks there's too much drug dealin' here on the reservation and wants to crack down. The Indian court usually handles Indian arrests, even off the reservation, but this time I hear they're gonna' make an example of Brady."

"Do you know who will be prosecuting?" Irv asked.

"Yeah. Dan Wessel. He came up from Phoenix just for Brady's case. They sent a judge up, too."

"I've heard of Wessel's reputation in Las Vegas." Irv turned to Sol. "Think we could drive into Parker to the courthouse and see if I can find him before tomorrow?"

"Sure," Sol said. He turned to Wanda. "Do you mind? We'll be back soon."

"Please go ahead. Anything you can do to make tomorrow easier."

She walked over and kissed him on the mouth.

When the women heard the Cadillac turn onto the highway, Naomi said, "Are you in love with him?"

"Yes, I am." Wanda spoke without hesitation. "He's a wonderful man and very good to me. He's paying Irv to represent Brady."

"I get a feelin' he's rich, too." Naomi's black eyes gleamed.

"He's well off." Wanda stared back at her sister.

"Wanna' tell me where you've been all these years?"

Wanda took a deep breath. "I've been in Las Vegas working as a dancer-stripper. I love my work, I make good money, and I'm generally happy now that Sol has come into my life."

Naomi was silent.

Wanda continued. "I don't make any apologies for the life I have now. I wanted to get away from the reservation. There was nothing here for me. I didn't want to marry Big Bill. I knew our father would insist eventually."

"Iris always loved Bill," Naomi said.

"Is she happy?"

"Who knows? She's crazy about him. When he gets drunk and beats her up, she forgives him the next day."

Wanda was startled. "Can't you do something about that?"

Naomi shook her head. "He's head man now that his father is gone."

Both women sat in silence for a long time. Eventually, Naomi rose and went to the kitchen to prepare the evening meal. Wanda followed. They fell into an ancient routine. Without words, they worked harmoniously, heating fry bread and beans and placing plump, yellow ears of corn into a pot of boiling water. Just as they had the large table set and everything ready, they heard a car pull into the yard. Through the front window, Wanda recognized the old rusted-blue Chevy belonging to Big Bill.

Nick

*D*owntown at the Calendar Club, Nick and Tony finished counting the day's take. Tony walked in front of the camera like he always did when Nick counted the last stack. Nick did not slip any bills into his vest this time. At Tony's surprised look, Nick barely shook his head. Tony locked the money in the safe for the morning's Brink's pickup. Nick turned out the lights and held the cage door open while Tony locked the count room.

"Come into my office a minute," Nick said. He nodded to Eddie at the bar, and Violet, balancing a tray of drinks on her way to the Pit, gave him a smile. Nick unlocked his office door and said, "Have a seat."

Tony sat in the chair, stomach filling his lap.

Nick sat down, swinging his legs to the top of his desk. "Carlo is aware that money is missing before it gets back East. Ace warned me I had to come up with a name of the guilty party this week. I wonder if you have any ideas?"

Tony began to sweat. "Jesus, Nick. What we gonna' do? You and me are the only ones that could really skim." He took a handkerchief from his back pocket and wiped his gleaming forehead.

"We need to give up someone. You know, somebody *is* stealing off the top, besides us."

Tony shook his head. "How could they? We are the only ones with keys."

"Has your key ever been out of your possession?"

Tony searched his memory. "Nope. I always keep it in my locked desk drawer."

"Where do you keep your desk key?"

"On my car ring."

"Have you loaned your car to anyone?"

Tony's face answered the question.

"Who?" Nick demanded.

"Eddie."

"Christ, man, when?"

"Several months ago." Tony wiped his forehead again.

Nick sat back in his chair. So it was Eddie who'd been doing the extra dipping that brought the amount taken to the attention of the bosses back East. But Eddie was the nephew of one of those big bosses, and his word would carry more weight with the family than Nick's.

"I just thought I should let you know before I have my meeting with Ace. He's been sent out to resolve the problem."

"Oh Christ! You think he's gonna' whack us?" Tony's voice faltered.

"No, I don't. But I have to give him a name, and I'm gonna' give him Eddie's. We have to stop skimming, at least, for a while. If we get out of this, we need to be less greedy. A smaller amount would probably be overlooked."

"Yeah, okay, Nick." Tony's stomach heaved. He continued to sweat and wipe his brow.

"Good night, Tony." Nick dismissed him.

"Yeah, 'night, Nick." Tony struggled up and hurriedly left the office.

Nick wondered if he was scared enough to run. He was hoping he was. That way, when he gave Tony's name to Ace, it would be believable. No way was he going to give up Eddie. He really hated to do this, but it was a matter of survival. He'd been shook up by Sol Wolfe's warning. He knew he had to act quickly.

He'd be a hell of a lot more careful from now on. Maybe he could find a cheaper convalescent home for his wife. That would ease finances considerably. And then he would decide what to do about Eddie.

Alan

$\mathcal{A}$lan backed out of his garage and headed downtown. He was meeting a friend of Lou's. He usually didn't do this, but Lou assured him the guy wanting to make a buy was okay. She said to look for a man wearing a red baseball cap. Entering North Las Vegas, the rough part of town, he drove into Washington Street, parked in front of a 7-Eleven, got out, and locked his car. He glanced nervously at a group of black men laughing on the corner. He could hear Otis Redding's "Sittin' on the Dock of the Bay" blaring out of a nearby house. Touching the plastic bag in his pocket, he walked south for a block and spotted a guy with a red cap.

Alan sauntered up to him. "Hi. Do we have a mutual friend?"

The black man nodded. "Lou," he spoke quietly.

"She said you wanted a half ounce. Did she tell you what I get for it?"

"Yeah, two thousand."

"You got the dough with you?"

"Yep."

"Let's see the money," Alan said.

The man put his hand in his pocket and pulled out a white envelope. Alan could see the money sticking out. It was passed over, and Alan began counting it.

"Hey, man, give me the stuff." The man rocked up on his toes.

125

"After I count this." Alan didn't look up. When he finished, he took the baggy from his pocket and handed it to the man.

The black man stuck his finger in the white substance and licked the end. "Yup."

Then he pulled a gun from his pocket and pointed it straight at Alan. "You're under arrest for selling illegal substances," the black man said.

Alan looked shocked. "Hey, that's not funny. Put the gun away."

Suddenly, two other men, one in uniform, appeared with guns drawn. One of them said, "This ain't no joke. You're under arrest. You have the right to remain silent." He proceeded to state the Miranda rights to Alan.

The uniformed cop took the money, handed it to the black plainclothesman, and handcuffed Alan's hands behind his back.

It all happened so fast, Alan's head was swimming. "You entrapped me. This isn't legal."

"We didn't do shit to you. You entrapped yourself," the other cop said. "Your friend, Lou, gave you up 'cause she's been busted. Think we'll pay a visit to your home. We might find some interesting stuff there."

They led him to the unmarked car down the street and put him in the back seat.

Alan's throat felt thick as he tried to swallow. He began to shake, handcuffs jangling. This couldn't be happening. He needed to call Sol. Then he remembered Sol was out of town with Wanda on some Indian reservation. Suzanne. He had planned to meet her after the show. Oh my God! Parts of his life flashed before his eyes. He saw himself graduating from college, standing at a twenty-one table in the casino, and then behind bars. Damn Lou! She had betrayed him. He had made a wrong decision in trusting her. What a mess he was in now.

Iris

*I*ris jumped from the car and ran up the steps, leaping over the missing one, and fell into Wanda's arms. They held each other for a long moment, eyes squinted, neither speaking.

Finally, Wanda pulled back and looked into her sister's face. Iris was still beautiful despite the remainder of a bluish bruise underneath her right eye. Tears rolled down her cheeks. Long silky hair, inherited by all the Moon girls, hung down her back. Iris was the tiny one, taking after their grandmother.

Beyond, in the yard, Wanda saw Big Bill unfold his wide body from the car. She met his cold eyes. He stared until she looked away.

"Where have you been?" Iris asked. "Why didn't you call me?"

Wanda felt a small pang of guilt for her favorite sister's pain. "I'm sorry, honey, for not letting you know. I just wanted to be completely on my own."

"But you came back. For Brady." There was no jealousy in her voice.

"Yes."

"How did you know?"

"I had a dream visitation from Father. I was instructed to return."

"Yes, Father would visit you. You were his favorite. Thank God you're home." Iris hugged her again, and they walked arm in arm into the house.

After Iris had greeted Naomi with a hug, she turned to Wanda. "How did you get here? How long can you stay? You haven't said where you've been."

Wanda laughed. "Slow down, Iris. I'll get to all that."

Big Bill came inside, slamming the screen door.

"Hello, Bill," Wanda said.

He nodded to her and sat down in the big recliner by the door.

"We're all waiting with great anticipation, Wanda. You have our ear," Naomi said, even though she'd already heard the story.

Wanda told them briefly of her life in Las Vegas for the last seven years. When she said she made her living as a stripper, Iris interrupted, "Wanda, you don't." Her eyes were big, and she broke into a grin.

Big Bill's eyes slid over Wanda like a coyote looking for a waterhole.

She told Iris about Sol and Irv, that they were in town right now, talking to the prosecuting attorney.

"Oh, Lord, I hope they can help," Iris lamented. "Brady is so rebellious. We can't do a thing with him."

Bill spoke for the first time. "So your boyfriend's paying the lawyer to defend Brady?"

Wanda nodded.

"Won't do no good. They're gonna' make an example of 'im."

"We'll see," Naomi said sternly. "Now don't be puttin' a bad spin on the hearing tomorrow."

"If by some miracle they do get Brady off, he's still gonna' be punished by the tribal council." Bill folded his hands across his chest.

"What do you mean?" Wanda asked, alarmed.

"I meant just what I said." Big Bill stood and slammed out the screen door.

Iris's smile vanished.

Naomi explained. "Don't you remember? The tribal council will decide on some sort of punishment. Usually, it's staying thirty-six hours out in the desert without food. Whatever it is, it will be better for Brady than going to the white man's jail."

Wanda had forgotten the tribal rituals, had put them out of her mind.

"Like the time he was caught stealing from a local liquor store. He was sentenced to three days and nights in the desert in 115-degree temperature, with only a canteen of water."

The three women sat in chairs at the table in silence.

"He survived that challenge. Brady will be all right." Changing the subject, Wanda put her hand on Iris's belly. "When's the baby due?"

"Four months."

"Do you know yet if it's a boy or girl?"

"No, Bill is against an ultrasound. We'll take whatever we get." She smiled, clasping Wanda's hand.

They saw Jackson's truck kicking up dirt as he came down the road. He stopped in the yard with a screech of brakes, got out and began talking to Big Bill. Wanda could see the two men, smoking cigarettes, cowboy boots propped side by side on the bumper of the '55 Ford truck. Jackson was tall and lean, just as she remembered him. His hair now gray, his sharp cheekbones and hawk-nose proclaimed his mixed-Indian heritage of Navaho and Chemehuevi.

Bill's body had become stocker. Thick arms and legs reminded Wanda of clubs. Bill was predominantly Mohave Indian, and the Mohaves were built like refrigerators. She shuddered at the thought of his huge fists connecting with her sister's face.

The women continued to watch through the large window as another dust cloud formed down the lane and the Cadillac pulled in beside the truck. Sol and Irv got out and introduced themselves. Jackson smiled and shook hands. Big Bill did not. He stood apart, his face like marble. Wanda saw Jackson's hand on Sol's shoulder. Something seemed to please him. He patted Irv on the back. In a few minutes the four tromped into the house.

Wanda introduced Iris to Sol and Irv.

"Nice to meet both of you," she said, her lovely mouth curved.

"Likewise," Irv said.

"It's a pleasure, Iris. I've heard so much about you from Wanda," Sol lied.

Iris turned her sweet smile on her sister, and Wanda did her best to appear deserving of it.

"Welcome home, Wanda," Jackson greeted her.

She smiled and thanked him.

"Have a seat, gentlemen. Tell 'em what ya' just told me, Sol." Jackson took a chair from the table, turned it around and sat astride it like on a horse.

Sol and Irv sat on the couch, and Bill returned to the recliner.

"We had an eventful couple of hours," Sol explained. "We got the attorney to agree to a lesser charge." Sol looked at Wanda first, then turned his gaze on Naomi and Iris.

"What lesser charge?" Wanda asked.

Irv took over. "The charge now is simple possession, which means Brady won't do jail time. A fine of $3000 to the court and three years probation will be recommended." Irv didn't mention how much money it really cost Sol.

"But Brady doesn't have $3000, nor do any of us." Iris' smile could come and go like a rainbow.

"My agreement with Wanda is that I would pay the fine," Sol said.

"But what if the judge don't go for it?" Naomi asked.

"The prosecuting attorney will recommend probation," Irv said. "The judge will go along."

"You are a mighty generous man, Sol. Wanda is a lucky woman." Jackson grinned.

"Yes. Thank you, Sol." Wanda threw him a grateful look.

"We all thank you." Naomi gave him a rare smile.

"Where I come from, we do what is necessary for family," Sol replied.

"And where would that be? Where you come from?" This was the first Bill had spoken.

"I'll go into that another time. Right now, I'd like to get out of these clothes and into something more comfortable." Sol turned toward Jackson. "Mind if we use your bathroom to change?"

Jackson jumped up. "Sure, sure. It's down the hall."

Sol and Irv went out to the Cadillac to get shorts and tee-shirts. Naomi and Iris went to the kitchen to heat up the food. Wanda, feeling Big Bill's eyes on her, joined her sisters.

Jackson put his feet up on the coffee table. "Boy, those two are some wheeler-dealers. Think I ought to take lessons from them. Whatcha' think, Bill?"

"If I was to say what I think, you wouldn't like it. So, I'll just say money talks."

"Sheeit! You're right about that, man. Ooowee...! Wait 'till Brady hears how those two got him off."

"He's still gotta' take his punishment from the tribal council," Bill said.

Jackson's exuberance suddenly waned. "Yeah, I guess."

When Sol and Irv finished changing, Naomi called everyone to dinner. The seven sat around the old wooden table, eating the browned fry bread, pinto beans and buttered corn on the cob.

After they had eaten their fill, Jackson cut up a huge watermelon into slices. Just as they finished, several cars and trucks roared down the lane, parking in the field next to the house. Clouds of dust swirled like desert devils. The squealing of children filled the air when they tumbled from the vehicles. Dogs barked as they jumped from truck beds. Naomi and Jackson's children and grandchildren stomped up the steps. The tribe was here. In spite of Bill's stony presence, Wanda felt she was being welcomed home. And best of all, tomorrow she would get to see her little brother set free.

Suzanne

*S*uzanne put the finishing touches on her makeup, adjusted her headdress, fluffed her feathered boa, and walked to the wings in preparation for her entrance with twenty-four other showgirls. They were standing all dressed identically, in a long line backstage in order of their appearance onstage. They ranged in height from 5 foot 9 inches to 6 feet tall. With three-inch heels they towered above the corps of dancers.

Considered too tall to be a dancer in a Vegas show, a showgirl's main purpose was to walk regally around the stage, supporting elaborate headdresses. Many were accomplished dancers but were stuck in the showgirl category.

A blue-eyed brunette next to Suzanne nudged her elbow. "I haven't seen you at any of the high-roller parties, lately," she whispered. "What happened?"

Suzanne whispered back, "I'm hoping they've overlooked me. I couldn't be happier about it."

"But you're giving up a C-note every time. Doesn't that hurt your life style?"

"I couldn't care less about the money. I hate those parties."

The showgirl shrugged. "I couldn't do without the extra money."

The stage manager motioned for them to watch for their cues. The first girl in line walked smoothly on stage, immediately followed by the next, until all had skimmed across the stage to their positions. The only thing Suzanne had to remember was to smile. By the time the show was over, her jaws ached. After the showgirls left the stage and returned to the dressing room for three more costume changes, it was time for the finale, and the showgirls actually got to kick their legs like the Rockettes. For Suzanne, that was the only strenuous dancing involved in the entire show. The audience applauded, and she felt the familiar rush of adrenaline and excitement that being onstage always held.

Backstage, she sat before the mirror, taking off the heavy makeup and double layer of false eyelashes. Alan hadn't called today so she didn't know if he would be waiting for her at the stage door. In fact, this was unusual. He called every day. He almost always waited for her after work and drove her home.

The gorgeous brunette, Faye, plopped down beside Suzanne. "God, that was boring. Don't you think Tommy could come up with more interesting moves for us instead of just standing around for half of the show?" Tommy was their choreographer. There was a running feud between the dancers and the showgirls. The showgirls wanted more dance steps to perform, and the dancers didn't want the extra competition.

"I don't think our lobby is very effective," Suzanne said as she wiped the cold cream from her face.

"Girl, we need a more persuasive voice. Any ideas?"

"Not much we can do about it, Faye. I have a feeling

the politics are set in cement."

"I never saw a situation that couldn't be negotiated and improved with a little sexual inducement." Faye winked at her.

"Honey, Tommy likes his boys. Who were you thinking of seducing?" Suzanne giggled.

"I was thinking of Brett Wallis, the director. Why not go to the top? And I like being on top. He sure is cute. And he likes the ladies."

"From what I hear, Brett is a pretty popular man."

"Can't blame a girl for trying. I hear he never turns down an offer."

Suzanne finished dressing into her street clothes. "Good luck, Faye. We do need someone to represent us."

"I'll let you know if I have any success. And how he performs. In bed, that is."

The women left the dressing room, giggling. They parted at the stage door, and Suzanne looked around for Alan. After waiting by the guard station for five minutes, she unlocked her car and drove home. Her disappointment was not a surprise. She was definitely in love for the first time. It was wonderful, blissful, but also anxious for her at times, and she worried about their future together. Alan made her feel like a complete woman. The only dark spot in her happiness was the knowledge that eventually she would have to tell him about the high-roller parties. Miraculously, she hadn't been called in weeks.

Suzanne parked alongside Wanda's Carmen Ghia. The phone was ringing as she put the key in the door and went into the apartment.

"Hello," Suzanne said breathlessly.

"Hi, honey, it's Alan. Stay calm, but I have bad news. I'm being held in the downtown lockup at the Las Vegas Police Station. I want you to call my uncle's lawyer, Irving Samuels, immediately. Look it up in the book. Tell his office that I need his help. He's with Sol and Wanda in Arizona."

Suzanne was confused. "What do you mean lockup? Police Station? What's happened?"

Alan spoke curtly. "Listen to me. I've been arrested for selling drugs. I only have this one phone call. You must call Irving Samuels. Do you understand?" Not waiting for an answer, Alan said, "I have to go now. I love you."

Suzanne felt tears pushing at the edges of her lids. Then the line was dead. Her hand trembled as she replaced the receiver. It had to be a mistake. Alan wouldn't do anything illegal. Drugs? Of course, the sleeping pills and uppers he gave her didn't count. They were prescription. At least, she thought they were. Besides, everyone in Vegas took pills. Downers to sleep and uppers to wake up.

My God! Alan was in trouble! As the full realization of his troubles seeped into her mind, tears rolled down her cheeks, and her fingers shook as she opened the yellow pages of the phone book.

Brady

Brady stood before the judge, head held high, long coarse hair tied in pony tail. Deep-set, black eyes looked defiantly at the man on the bench. Irv had a hell of a time convincing him that pleading guilty to the lesser charge of possession was a better deal than trying to fight the original charge of selling illegal substances. Finally, Sol persuaded him by threatening to pull out and leave him to fight his own battle.

Wanda, Sol, Naomi, Iris, and Jackson were all in the front row. Irv stood beside Brady. Wanda had caught Brady's eye a couple of times. He looked angry. Perhaps at Sol. Sol had said he had to come down hard on Brady's expectations.

"How do you plead, Brady Moon?" the judge asked.

"He pleads guilty, your honor, to the reduced charge of possession." Irv's strong voice could be heard to the back of the courtroom.

"I see Mr. Wessel recommended probation with a fine." The judge looked up. "Are you in agreement, Brady Moon?"

"Yes."

"Mr. Moon, in my courtroom, you will address me as Your Honor."

Brady hesitated. Then he said, "Yes, Your Honor."

"Very well, Brady Moon, you will be fined $3000 and receive three years probation. The fine can be paid at the clerk's desk outside. Are you prepared to pay the fine, Mr. Moon?"

"Yes, Your Honor, he is," Irv answered.

The judge passed the papers to the court clerk and pronounced Brady free to go.

The three sisters embraced. Brady was led out the courtroom by Irv, and everyone else joined them in the hallway. Naomi and Iris hugged him. Wanda stood aside. Jackson pumped his back.

Brady released his sisters and looked at Wanda. "'Bout time you came home, Little Dove." He slid his arms around her shoulders, tucking his fingers in her long hair and pulled her to him.

Wanda's tears dampened his shirt. She stepped back and looked into Brady's face. "You look so much like our father."

"Well, that's good, since I'm his son." Brady smiled for the first time. His face opened and his eyes gleamed.

"I think this calls for a celebration. Why don't we adjourn across the street at The Corral for a beer?" Jackson suggested.

"Sounds like a winner," Brady agreed.

Wanda looked at Sol.

"We'll join you in a few minutes," Sol said. He and Irv headed for the clerk's office.

Brady and his family walked across the street to the bar and piled into a large booth in the back. Jackson ordered two pitchers of Coors.

Brady slid in beside Wanda, with Iris on the other side.

"Brady, I'm only going to say this one time." Wanda looked him straight in the eye. "It's time you got your life together."

"Yeah, Sis, I got a lot to thank you for," Brady said as he buzzed her cheek.

"No, Brady, let's be clear. Sol paid for everything today. He paid for Irv's time and for us to travel here from Vegas. He is investing in your future. One that we both hope you will embrace in a more responsible manner. He may not be here to bail you out if there's a next time. Do you understand me?"

The waitress brought the pitchers, and Brady poured beer for everyone. "So, you want me to thank your boyfriend?" He looked at her, his dark eyes full of ancient secrets.

"That would be polite, Brady. But I'm not asking you to. You have to decide yourself."

"You know, Brady," Naomi said, "You could have been a lot worse off if Sol and Irv hadn't come down here and got involved in your problem."

Brady stared into his beer.

Sol and Irv came through the swinging doors. They walked to the booth and slipped in beside Jackson.

"Brady, you have to report monthly to your probation officer, Molly Reilly, here in Parker. If you stay out of trouble, I can probably get your probation time reduced to eighteen months," Irv explained.

"You guys are regular fuckin' magicians, aren't you?" Brady looked from Irv to Sol.

"We don't speak that way in front of our women." Sol's stone-gray eyes met Brady's as he poured beer for Irv and himself.

No one said a word. Jackson's hand on his beer mug froze in mid-air. The three sisters stared down into their beer.

Brady drained his glass and poured seconds for himself. He looked across the table at Sol. "Guess I owe you some thanks for gettin' me out of this jam. I know you didn't do it for me, but I still thank you. And I apologize to my sisters for my lack of manners." He smiled charmingly at the three women.

"You're right. I didn't do it for you." Sol lifted his glass toward Brady.

Everyone breathed a sigh of relief, and the subject was changed. They talked of the crops and the monthly government checks that were in the mail for each Indian on the reservation. Finally, the two pitchers were emptied, and Sol suggested he get everyone home because they had to return to Vegas.

Wanda was surprised because they hadn't discussed it, but said nothing. She expected Sol had had about enough of her clan.

Brady and Irv climbed in the back of the Cadillac, and Naomi and Iris rode with Jackson in the truck.

During the drive back, Wanda asked, "Why are we going back so soon?"

"I'll tell you after we return to the motel." Sol kept his eyes on the road, following Jackson.

Back at Naomi and Jackson's home, biding her sisters and Brady good-bye was painful. She was reminded then why she hadn't gone back all these years. There were just too many undercurrents and implications. But she promised to stay in touch. It was hardest to leave Iris.

Her sister clung to her. "Please come back soon, Wanda. I need to talk to you sometimes."

"You can call me collect anytime you need to talk." She held Iris close. "If you need help, I'll come," she whispered in her ear.

She met Naomi's black eyes and reached for her, clasping her tightly. Naomi's arms lay loosely around Wanda's shoulders.

Brady swept her into his arms and kissed her on the lips. "Don't stay away so long, Little Dove." He held her for a long time.

Jackson patted her arm, and Big Bill avoided her, slamming out the screen door.

She waved good-bye as Sol drove down the dirt lane. A deep sigh escaped her lips. She knew she could never return to live on the reservation.

Once back in their motel rooms in Parker with Irv installed next door, Wanda could contain herself no longer.

"What's so important that we have to return to Vegas tomorrow?"

Sol told her to sit down. "Alan's in jail for selling drugs. When we were in Parker, Irv called his office, and Suzanne had left a frantic message for him. I called

Suzanne. So it seems your family isn't the only one that gets busted." He ran his fingers through his thick gray hair.

"My God! Is Alan all right?"

"I don't know. Suzanne was terribly upset. I was able to calm her down and told her we'd be back tomorrow."

Wanda put her hand over her mouth. "I can't imagine Alan selling drugs. Can you?"

"Alan is capable of anything. He's been a risk taker ever since he was a small boy."

"Are you saying you think the charges are valid?"

"Honey, I don't know until I talk to him and the police. Irv's secretary says he's being held on $75,000 bail. Must be some heavy stuff he was selling."

Wanda went to Sol and pulled him close. "Darling, I'm so sorry that you weren't in town when Alan needed you."

"That's the breaks. I was here when you needed me."

"I haven't properly thanked you for today. Think you could handle a little appreciation?" She ran warm hands down his chest, sliding her fingers inside his slacks.

"I think that's just what I need, my love."

Violet and Ruby

Violet was drinking her second cup of coffee when Ruby came shuffling into the kitchen, rubbing her eyes. She wasn't bleaching her hair anymore, and four inches of dark roots showed near her scalp.

"Morning," Ruby mumbled as she poured herself the last cup and pulled her blue housecoat tighter around her breasts.

"Morning," Violet said, eyes down.

Once the coffee began to make her more alert, Ruby looked closely at her roommate. Violet's eyes were swollen. "What's wrong?"

"Nothing." Violet looked down at the pattern of the tablecloth. She traced the red paisley swirl with her forefinger.

"Now, I know something is. I haven't lived with you for two years and not know when something's bothering you."

"I can't talk about it." Violet looked up and met Ruby's eyes. Tears welled up and dripped over the thick fringe of her lashes.

"You can certainly talk to me about it. I'm not gonna' say a word to anyone."

Violet felt herself giving in. "I think Nick's in deep trouble. I'm afraid for him." She wiped tears from her cheeks.

Ruby nodded. "Go on."

"I think he's been stealing from the casino, and the bosses back East are on to him, but he doesn't seem to think he's in danger. And the other night, we met with this scary character at the Village Pub. He told Nick that he would be held responsible for the loss and gave him a deadline to come up with the guilty party."

Ruby sat in thought for a moment. "What makes you think Nick is doing the skimming?"

"I work there. I see who has access and who doesn't. Only he and the accountant, Tony, ever count the money." Violet pulled a tissue from her purple terrycloth robe and blew her nose.

"Perhaps it's a Pit Boss or one of the dealers."

Violet shook her head. "No, it's a lot of money. They wouldn't have access to that amount."

"How much are we talking about?"

Violet looked up. "In the neighborhood of $200,000."

Ruby whistled. "Wow! Your boyfriend does it big. I'll say that for him."

"It's been going on for quite a while," Violet said. "Over several months."

"Perhaps Nick ought to try and pay it back."

"He claims he isn't the one. I think he's going to blame Tony." Violet started to cry again.

Ruby came around the counter and put her arm across her roommate's shoulders. "But you think Nick's stolen the money, right?"

Violet nodded through her tears.

"You know, honey, you may be in danger, too. If I were you, I'd leave Nick alone and get a job elsewhere. You know too much already."

"I can't. I love him. I want to help him."

"I know that, but sometimes we can't help others until we help ourselves. I'm learning that lesson right now."

"I understand what you're saying, Ruby, but I can't leave him. He needs me."

Ruby went to the counter and dropped two pieces of bread in the toaster. She took eggs from the refrigerator and broke four into a frying pan. "Well, let's have some breakfast. Things are bound to look better after that."

"Ruby, please don't discuss this with Craig. I swore to Nick I wouldn't say a word to anyone."

"Don't worry, honey. It will be just between us. But Craig could be a big help if you'd just trust him." Ruby wished she could talk to him about it. But she would honor Violet's wishes, at least for now.

Sol, Suzanne and Alan

When Sol and Wanda returned to Vegas, Suzanne was waiting at the apartment. Her red eyes were nearly swollen shut. Sol put his arms around her, and she cried on his shoulder.

"I've been crazy, not being able to see him or talk to him except that one phone call."

Wanda slipped an arm around her waist. "Try to stay calm. Sol will make his bail, and he'll be out today. Hold it together, honey." She gave Suzanne a hug before they left for the police station.

Sol hurriedly drove the ten blocks and parked the Rolls in the police lot. He looked around nervously, trying to find a safe place for the car, and finally took up two parking spaces. They immediately went to the clerk's office, where he read the police report and the charges, and he paid the bail of 75,000 dollars. The charge was selling illegal substances and operating a meth-amphetamine lab, pretty serious stuff. They had raided Alan's home and found the lab paraphernalia, plus several baggies of speed, all processed, cut and ready for sale.

Suzanne and Sol watched as the policeman brought Alan down the hallway. Alan had been in a holding tank for two days and nights. His light green shirt was wrinkled and dirty, and the pants he wore were stained with food. Two days of beard growth gave his handsome features a tough look. Suzanne had never seen him before in soiled clothes.

"Thanks for bailing me out, Sol," Alan said, his face white and haggard.

Sol nodded.

Alan looked at Suzanne and reached out to put his hand on her shoulder. She drew back very slightly, then stepped forward and hugged him. He smelled of vomit, and musty odors clung to his clothing and hair, so unlike the immaculate man she knew. She held her breath and prayed she wouldn't gag. Finally, Alan released her, and Sol held the glass door open. They walked out to the Rolls, Suzanne climbed in the back and Alan slid into the passenger seat.

"Apparently from what the police report says, they didn't get the wrong house," Sol said dryly.

Alan ran fingers through his dark hair. "God, Sol, I'm sorry. I never meant to get caught. I've always been so careful." He looked back at Suzanne, his eyes asking forgiveness.

"You obviously weren't careful enough. Whatever possessed you to make and sell speed, anyway?" His uncle kept his eyes on the road.

"I found a recipe on an old college leaflet stuck in one of my chemistry books. I knew I could cook up some pretty good stuff and make a lot of money."

"If you needed money, you should have come to me," Sol said.

"I didn't need money, Unc, I just wanted to make

a lot. Like you and Dad."

"You picked a hell of a way to do it. I hope you realize the jam you're in. Not sure if I can get you out of this one without jail time." They were at a stop sign, and Sol took the opportunity to glare at Alan.

"You think they'll send me to jail?" Alan asked. "I can't do time. I wouldn't survive."

"Irv says for a first offender, you'll probably get ten to twelve. Maybe get paroled in five or six."

Alan's face turned from white to gray.

Sol left the strip and headed out Flamingo Blvd. "What about your mother and father? Are you going to tell them?"

"No, I can't tell Mom or Dad either. Can't we just keep this between us?"

"When you go to jail, Alan, it's going to be pretty hard to keep the news from them."

"As you always say, Unc, let's cross that bridge when we come to it. For now, I don't want them to know."

Suzanne was frozen in the backseat. She hadn't said a word as she listened to Alan and his uncle. Her world was crumbling around her. She almost felt as if she had lost a loved one. If Alan went to jail, what would that do to their relationship? And he said he couldn't survive there. What did that mean? Would he be killed? Large tears rolled silently down her cheeks. Her mouth quivered. Alan turned just then and saw her face.

"I'm so sorry, honey," he said.

Sol and Alan

*A*lan fixed two Scotches and handed one to Sol. They went out to sit on the covered patio. The sun was still midway in the sky, and the temperature had not yet reached 100 degrees. The trees around Alan's back yard hovered over cool shadows. Boots darted between Sol's legs and headed for the nearest bush.

"What are my options, Unc? Is there any way I can avoid jail?"

Sol put his feet up on the chaise lounge. "Irv says no. They're going to throw the book at you. You were operating a meth lab in your home. You had your merchandise packaged for sale. Because it's your first offense, you'll probably get ten, twelve years. With good behavior, you could get out in six, seven."

Elbows on the table, Alan covered his eyes with his palms. "I can't do it. I won't be alive to get paroled in six years. Some guy tries to use me for sex and I'm done.'"

Both men sat silently, sipping their drinks.

"There is another way. But it's a road of no return." Sol had a faraway look in his eyes as he spoke.

Alan looked up, "What's that?"

"You run. Go to another country, disappear with a new identify, and never return to the U.S."

Alan looked shocked. "I couldn't do that. I'd never see you or Mom or Dad again, not to mention Suzanne. Besides, I don't have the money to disappear."

Sol twirled the empty glass on the table. "A new identity and passport can be arranged. After you're settled, we could visit occasionally. Your father and I will make sure you have enough money to live the rest of your life, providing you live within reason and never get in trouble with the law again."

"My God!" Alan said. "You would do this for me?"

"Of course I'd do this for you. In spite of your lack of good judgment, I care about you very much. But Suzanne is another matter."

"What do you mean?"

"She may not want to go with you. Cut all her ties and disappear."

Alan remembered her stricken face in the car.

Sol looked down at his glass. "I think you know, you're the son I never had."

Alan sat with his chin in his hands. His gaze was level with his uncle's. "I know that. I feel closer to you, Uncle Sol, than I do to Dad. I guess I've always felt I was invincible. That nothing bad would happen to me. I've lived a charmed life, and I thought it would just go on and on." A tear spilled from the edge of one eye. Alan quickly wiped it away. "So what do you advise?"

"I can't advise you on this," his uncle said. "You must make your own decision."

"Do you think Suzanne would come with me, if I decide to go?"

Sol looked straight at Alan. "No, I don't. She's too fragile for a life on the run."

Alan shook his head. "I don't want a life without her. I've never met anyone I felt the same about."

"You got a lot of thinking to do, son. I can't help you with Suzanne. If you decide to go, let me know immediately. I need time to get a passport and new papers for you. Then we have to find a safe place and airline tickets in your new identity."

"But you'd lose your bail money if I don't show for the trial."

"In the big picture, that's not important."

The two men stood and went into the house. Alan pulled the drapes, leaving the house once again in quiet dimness. He moved toward his uncle and wrapped his arms around bulky shoulders. Sol returned the embrace.

Alan stepped back. "I can never thank you enough for your help. If I leave, I could never repay the money."

"My payment would be that you stay out of trouble and free of jail for the rest of your life. Think you could manage that?"

"Yeah, I think I could do that." But Alan wondered if he could stand that kind of low-risk life. He also couldn't help wondering if Suzanne loved him enough to go with him.

Violet and Nick

$\mathcal{N}$ick and Violet were having a glass of wine in his home in the Country Club Estates. They'd left the club around 2:00 a.m. with Eddie in charge, overnight. Nick had decided to contact Ace tomorrow and give up Tony. He sat quietly beside Violet.

"Nick, what's wrong?" She knew he was concerned about something. She guessed it had to do with the money stolen from the casino.

"Oh, I guess I'm just a little distracted, honey. Never mind me."

She pulled him to her. "I'd be happy to take your mind off any distraction right now."

He kissed her, and they walked up the spiral staircase to the bedroom.

⌒

Violet opened her eyes to an unfamiliar sound and squinted at the clock. 4:00 a.m. She looked over at Nick. He was sleeping next to her, his dark head on the silk pillowcase, arm flung across her tummy, his chest hairs black against the moonlit sheet. She lay still, listening. She heard a far-off siren, but nothing else. Moving slowly so as not to awaken him, she slipped from beneath his arm, stepped onto the soft rug, and headed for the bathroom. Half-way there, she remembered her birth control pill on the table in the den. She tiptoed down the hall, opened the door and closed it, so as not to disturb Nick. Looking out the windows, she thought she saw movement on the golf course. Nick had left the patio light on. There was a breeze, and the tall palms cast moving shadows across the green. The backlighting in the trees magnified the effect. She stood there daydreaming for a few moments, then turned to search for her pill box. Just then, she thought she heard another noise…in the house. She walked to the door and cocked her ear, her nakedness blending with the dark room. She didn't know why she continued to listen. Suddenly, a strange noise came from the bedroom down the hall. She continued to listen. She heard…Fitttttt…Fittttt…Fitttt…. She heard it three times, like the soft sound of a snake hissing. Instinct told her she was in danger! Violet quietly tiptoed to the desk and crept into the alcove, her heart pounding so hard she was sure it could be heard outside the room. Terrified, she began to shake. She didn't know how long she waited. Soon she heard footsteps on the marble stairs again, going down. Someone was going down less quietly than they came up.

It felt like she had been in the desk alcove an eternity, too frightened and paralyzed to move. After a while she unwound herself, cold and stiff. She moved toward the door. Another eternity passed as she listened. She quietly opened the door and walked down the hall, every nerve in her body alert. She entered the bedroom. She could see Nick on the silk sheet, dark splotches oozed across the pillowcase. His head was covered in blood. A giant hole had taken out most of his face. Above the bed was a Rorschach pattern of blood dripping down over the headboard. She pressed her hands to her mouth, forcing herself not to cry out. The smell of fresh blood flooded her nostrils, and she gagged several times. A deep sob escaped her throat and she laid her forehead on the edge of the blanket and her hand on Nick's wrist. No pulse. "No, No," she murmured. Swallowing the bile in her mouth, she got to her feet, grabbed her skirt, blouse and underwear from the closet hanger and hurriedly dressed. She scooped up her sandals and purse and walked down the circular stairs, feeling the coolness of the marble steps on her hot feet.

She looked across the room at the spider plant. Remembering what Nick had told her about it, she hurried over and lifted it out of the large pot. She saw a flat board underneath, which Nick said was a false bottom. A small tab appeared on one side and she pulled on it. It came away, revealing a beige canvas bag. Money was sticking out of the bag. She returned the plant to its place, crammed the money inside the bag, and held it securely in her arms. She headed for the back of the house and opened the glass door to the patio. Finding the door unlocked, she reached up and twisted out the light outside, burning her fingers.

Violet darted to the edge of the green, keeping well within the shadow of the trees. Moonlight shone brightly on the course. Her panic shortened her breathing, and she slowed to a walk. Moving stealthily behind the other mansions, she came to a path. Trotting down the dirt trail, she saw a street sign ahead. Maryland Parkway. She walked two blocks to a big shopping center and across the street she spied a taxi. Her waving arms caught the attention of the driver. He made a U-turn and pulled up beside her. She jumped into the back and caught her breath, clutching the bag.

The driver turned in his seat. "Lady, you all right?" Then he recognized her. "Violet," Craig said.

Violet fought back more tears. "Please, take me home."

"Sure thing. Are you in trouble? Can I help?"

"Yes, just take me home, Craig." Her burning fingers began to throb from the hot light bulb.

"On our way." He stepped on the gas and turned off the meter, calling in on his radio to the office. "I'm not feeling well. Going off duty for tonight." He thought possibly he didn't want a record of this ride. In ten minutes he stopped in front of the Desert Winds Apartments.

Violet started to open her purse, but Craig shook his head. "The drive's on me. You've been so good to Ruby, guess I can do a favor for you."

Violet didn't argue. "Thanks, Craig."

"Sure thing, honey. See ya' later."

Violet put her key in the door quietly so as to not wake Ruby. Leaning against the inside wall, she took her first deep breath since the nightmare began. Tears running down her cheeks, she closed her bedroom door before giving in to the sobs rising from her chest like a tsunami on the sea.

Violet

Violet sobbed for more than an hour. Her eyes were nearly swollen shut when the tears finally dried up. She continued to sob, soundlessly. When the hiccups started, she sat up and drank some water, banishing the sobs.

Nick was gone. She would never see him again. Her heart was torn apart. Never to feel his arms around her, his body next to hers. The pain threatened to engulf her once more. Taking deep breaths, she looked at the canvas bag on the foot of her bed. She untied the drawstring and dumped the bag upside down. Several packets of money fell out. One hundred-dollar bills were on top of each stack. She leafed through them; they were all one hundred-dollar bills! Close to fifty thousand dollars, when she counted it. Without a doubt Nick has stolen this money from the casino. Was that what the killers wanted? Or did they mean to punish him for stealing? Nick had said this was his emergency money. What should she do? Would they be looking for her? Probably. Several people at the casino knew she was his girlfriend. She sat for a moment, then went to the closet and pulled down a suitcase. She began methodically packing clothes. When she was finished, she took a note pad from her dresser and wrote:

Dear Ruby,

I'm so sorry I have to leave here. You may never hear from me again. Please keep the money and burn this note.

Tell no one of my leaving, except Craig. You were right; he is a good man.

Nick is dead. I am running for my life. If the police or anyone questions you, you know nothing. I would advise hiding this money for several months. Get out of this town, and spend it elsewhere. Don't attract attention by spending too much at once. Tell no one I gave it to you.

I have enclosed a note that you can show the police when they question you. This will explain my sudden departure and protect you. Remember, I told you that my aunt is ill with cancer and I have suddenly moved there to care for her.

Please stay sober, Ruby. I know you can do it.

Love, Violet

Then Violet wrote a second note.

Dear Ruby

I am moving to Long Beach to stay with my aunt for right now and later will get my own apartment and look for a job, when my aunt no longer needs my care. Please have my mail sent to Long Beach, CA c/o of General Delivery, until I get a permanent address. Would you please put in a change of address at the post office for me? Thanks.

I have enclosed a check for $200 for you to put the rest of my things in storage, as I didn't have a chance. You can mail the storage receipt to me care of General Delivery.

Thanks so much for helping me. Sorry I had to leave so abruptly and didn't get to say good bye. I'll be in touch.

Love, Violet

Violet counted out $10,000, put the money, the check, and the notes in a paper bag and tiptoed to Ruby's room. Her now light brown hair lay scattered over the pillow, her face clean of makeup. Quietly, Violet laid the paper bag on the bed.

She returned to her room, picked up her suitcase and the canvas bag and took a last look around the room. She left her key on the kitchen table, and went out of the apartment. Gray light was beginning to show in the eastern sky. Sunglasses in place to hide her swollen eyes, she walked to her car, threw her suitcase in the trunk, stashed the canvas bag under her spare tire, and backed out of the carport. The sun was just peeking over the horizon as Violet turned onto I-15 and headed north out of Las Vegas, Nevada.

Wanda and Suzanne

Wanda and Suzanne were at their kitchen table having a light breakfast of eggs and grapefruit.

Suzanne picked at her eggs. "I can hardly keep my mind on the cues onstage, I'm so worried about Alan."

"I think I understand what you're going through," Wanda said, "but you can leave the worrying to Alan and Sol. There isn't a damn thing you can do about this mess."

"I know you're right, but I can't help myself."

"Alan's still working, isn't he?"

Suzanne nodded. "The casino doesn't seem to care that he's been arrested. As long as it wasn't gambling-related. That's what his Pit Boss said."

Being Sol's nephew didn't hurt, Wanda thought.

"Alan has been so distracted lately. He doesn't even want to make love." Suzanne fiddled with her fork.

"That probably won't last long." Wanda didn't mention that Sol had told her about his offer for Alan to leave the country permanently. She did agree with Sol that Suzanne probably wouldn't do well in a life on the run.

Wanda turned on the television. She returned to the table and poured more coffee for herself and Suzanne.

The 11 a.m news was just beginning. The female anchor was reporting on a murder in the plush Las Vegas Country Club Estates.

"The murdered man has been identified as Nick Capela, the casino manager of the Calendar Club. He was found by the housekeeper when she came to work. Police say he was shot in the head. The killing occurred sometime between midnight and 4:00 a.m. this morning."

"My God! That's Violet's boyfriend," Wanda burst out. "You know, Ruby's roommate."

Suzanne came out of her funk and watched the screen. "Oh, my God!"

The reporter continued.

"There were no witnesses or any reported disturbances. The guards at the main gate said nothing unusual occurred. Speculation as to who might be responsible for the murder runs rampant. Apparently the ownership of the casino is unclear, so the police are having trouble tracking down the stockholders. Police say they have no leads at this time.

"In another part of the city..."

Wanda switched off the television and hurried down the hall to her bedroom.

Sol picked up the phone immediately. "Yes." He never identified himself.

"It's me. Have you heard the news about Nick Capela? It was just on the television."

"Yes, dear, I heard."

"Remember I told you that I met a waitress that works there. Violet Kandinsky? She was Nick's girlfriend. I hope she's okay."

Sol remembered the beautiful waitress that led him to Nick's office. "I wouldn't worry about her. She's probably fine. Whoever did it probably wasn't after her."

Wanda felt relieved. Sol always seemed to know about these things. "The other reason I called was the reporter said they were looking for the names of the casino stockholders."

"Don't worry about that either, love."

"Okay, how is Alan doing?"

"He's got a lot to think about. What he's going to do with the rest of his life."

"Yes, I don't envy him having to make that decision. Suzanne is still depressed and upset. I'm dropping her off at work on my way to the club."

"So you want me to send a cab for you after work?" Sol asked. "I don't think I'll be there, tonight."

"No, I can drive my car. See you later."

As she hung up, she hoped Sol was right about Violet not being in danger. Her thoughts turned to Suzanne. The last few days, she had begun distancing herself ever so slightly from Alan. Wanda noticed because Suzanne was asking for a ride to work every night, and Alan used to pick her up.

Ruby

$\mathcal{R}$uby opened her eyes and rolled over, one tiny foot edging off the mattress. She looked at the clock: 12 o'clock noon. Exhausted, she had gone to bed immediately after Craig dropped her off. Eager to pick up a few more customers before dawn, he hadn't come back. Lately, she'd felt tired and dragged out. Maybe she needed a checkup with her doctor.

Ruby threw back the covers and sat up. She spotted a brown paper bag on the end of the bed. When she opened it, she reached in and pulled out a stack of bills. Hundred-dollar bills! She stared at them in disbelief. She turned the bag upside down and more one hundred-dollar bills tumbled onto the bedspread. Two pieces of paper and a check also fell out.

Ruby picked up the notes and read them. Violet gone? Nick dead? Her morning foggy brain couldn't comprehend the full implications. She got out of bed, and the paper bag slipped to the floor. Stumbling down the hall, she looked into Violet's room. It was empty. Barefoot, she padded into the kitchen. Everything was quiet and neat as usual. She started the coffee, needing a cup before she could think straight. Standing at the sink, the full realization hit her, and she felt the beginning of panic rise from her belly and make its way to her chest, like a snake unwinding its tapered coils. Tears rolled down her cheeks. What would she do without

Violet to help her over the rough spots? She knew it was a selfish thought. What about Violet? Craig would know what to do. She picked up the phone and dialed.

"Hullooo…" Craig mumbled.

"It's Ruby," she said tearfully. "Can you come over right now?"

Craig came awake. "What's wrong?"

"I…I…think I want a drink. I need your help. Can you come?"

"Sure, honey, I'll be right there. Have a cup of coffee. I'll be there before you finish."

She saw her hand tremble as she replaced the phone. Luckily she didn't have any liquor in the apartment. She could keep herself from walking down to the 7-Eleven by not getting dressed. The percolator gurgled its final gulp, and she poured herself a hot cup. By the time she'd finished it, her hands were again steady. Just as she poured a second cup, Craig knocked. She opened the door and flew into his arms. "Oh, Craig! Violet's gone…"

Craig held her as she babbled out about the money and notes. He rubbed her back, soothing her as if she were a small child. Finally, he walked with her into the kitchen and poured himself a cup of coffee, one arm still around Ruby's waist.

"Where is the money?" Craig asked.

"In here," she said. They headed for her room. The money was strewn across the bed just as she had dumped it, bundles of hundred-dollar bills staring up at him. He had never seen so much money before. He seated Ruby on the end of the bed, put down his coffee, and knelt beside her. He picked up the two notes and read them as Ruby watched his face. He didn't look surprised. When he was finished, he counted the money. "Yup. Ten thousand, just like she said."

"But why: Where did she get it?" Ruby was on the verge of tears again.

"You know where it came from. Nick's casino. Evidently, she wanted you to have some of it. Listen to me, Ruby. Violet is absolutely right. The only way to keep this money is to put it away for now. No one must know you have it."

Ruby's eyes took on a glazed look. "But what if they come after me and find it?" Her voice quavered.

"I think we should hide it for the time being. Would you let me take it out of your apartment?"

Ruby nodded without hesitation. "What will you do with it?"

"I'll open a safe deposit box. Where no one but us can touch it. I think I ought to put it in my name. That way there is no connection to you. Is that all right?"

Ruby thought about what Craig had said. "Okay, I think that's a good idea." She swallowed noticeably. "Craig, I want a drink in the worst way. I can't imagine my life without Violet." She cried again.

He slid over on his knees and hugged her. "Baby, you have me. I think you should move in with me as soon as possible. You can't afford this rent with Violet gone."

She pulled back and looked into his face. "You want me to move in with you? You've never asked me before."

"I didn't ask because I knew you were close to Violet and wanted her company. But I intended to, eventually."

They looked at each other for a long time. Then Ruby said, "I'd love to live with you, Craig."

He stood. "Now, why don't you get dressed, and we'll go out to breakfast. But first, we'll go directly to the bank and unload this money. I can't go driving around with it in my cab. It's too risky."

Ruby brushed away the tears that had fallen on her cheek. "Could we climb into bed for a minute? I just want you to hold me."

Craig picked up the money and put it back in the bag. He took some matches from his pocket, picked up Violet's first note and struck a match. Catching a corner of the white paper, he held it over the ashtray until the flame burned it into thick, curly ashes. The other note and the check he placed under the lamp on the table. Then he turned to Ruby and pulled back the covers. She crawled under and Craig slipped off his shoes and climbed in beside her. His arm covered her breasts, and he gently kissed her neck. His tongue licked her soft skin, and then he began to nibble on her throat. Ruby moaned, and they started shedding their clothes.

Eddie, the Bartender

$\mathcal{T}$ ony and Eddie left the count room, and Tony locked the door behind them. Tony was doing the count this morning because Nick said he wouldn't be in until late.

Eddie figured Nick and Violet were spending the day together since she hadn't come to work, either. Must be tough duty for Nick, spending the day naked between the sheets with that gorgeous woman.

Eddie went behind the bar and poured two fingers of Wild Turkey. He watched Tony head for Nick's office, then turned his back and drank the whiskey down in one gulp. Drinking on duty was not tolerated by Nick, but when he was gone, Eddie did what he wanted. He wiped down the bar and stacked glasses in hot soapy water. Business was slow. Just a few tourists at the tables and slots.

The morning continued hot, sultry, and slow. For once, the air conditioner could handle the smoke in the casino. Eddie was mixing a drink when a tall plain-clothesman stepped up to the bar. He pulled a badge from his pocket for Eddie to see.

"I'm Detective Clayton from Las Vegas Homicide. Who is the person in charge here?"

Eddie looked at the badge. "Uh…Tony Rivera is on duty right now. Our manager isn't in this morning."

"Could I speak with Mr. Rivera?" the detective asked.

"Sure, but can I help you? I'm the bartender, Eddie Bono."

"I need to talk to the man in charge."

"Okay. I'll take you to him." Eddie put down the bottle and came from behind the bar. He escorted the detective down the corridor to the office in back and knocked loudly.

"Yes," Tony answered.

"Tony, a policeman is here to see you." The door clicked open, and the two men entered.

Tony stood up behind his desk. "What can I do for you?" Tony asked.

Again Detective Clayton pulled his badge from his pocket and identified himself. "Is Nick Capela, the manager of this casino?"

Tony looked from Eddie to the detective. "He isn't here right now."

Eddie stood behind the policeman, raising his brows to Tony.

"Mr. Capela was murdered in his home early this morning."

Tony was stunned. He fell back in his chair. "My God!"

Eddie, too, sat down.

The detective noted the reactions of the two men, and he seated himself in the remaining chair.

"When did you last see him?"

"Why...he was here yesterday." Tony reached up and rubbed his forehead. "Yes, he left the casino around 2:00 a.m. this morning."

Detective Clayton nodded. "Did you see him leave?"

"No. Actually I didn't come in until eight this morning, my usual time. But Eddie was here."

The policeman turned to Eddie. "You saw him leave?"

Eddie nodded.

"Did he leave the club alone?"

Eddie hesitated. Shit, he hated to get Violet in trouble. The cop hadn't said they found two bodies. "One of the cocktail waitresses left at the same time. But I don't know if they left together."

"What's her name?" Detective Clayton took out a notebook.

Eddie gave him Violet's name.

"Do you have an address for her?" the policeman asked.

"I'll look it up," Tony volunteered as he opened a drawer and pulled out a file titled EMPLOYEES. He found Violet's address, wrote it on a slip of paper, and gave it to the detective.

Looking at the slip of paper, the detective asked, "What was the relationship of Miss Kandinsky and Mr. Capela?"

"They dated," Tony said.

"Did Nick have any enemies that you know of?" He turned to include Eddie in the question.

Eddie shook his head. "I can't think of anyone that would be considered an enemy."

The detective addressed both men. "Anybody threaten Mr. Capela that you know of, or were there any incidents in the casino lately?"

Eddie shook his head firmly. "No, nothing unusual has happened here in the casino. Just the usual losers."

"Eddie's right. This is a small casino. We rarely have any high rollers or excitement here."

Detective Clayton took his card from his pocket and laid it on the desk. "If you think of anything that might be of help, please call me." He stood to leave.

Tony unlocked the door. The policeman and Eddie left. They walked back into the casino-bar area, and Eddie went behind the bar. One of the waitresses was standing at the end of the bar.

"Eddie, where you been? I got drink orders to fill." She began reciting the drinks, and Eddie started mixing them.

"When does your shift end?" Detective Clayton asked Eddie.

"I'm going home in a few minutes. I've been here since one this morning."

Detective Clayton nodded and left the casino.

When Eddie finished mixing the last drink for the waitress's tray, he picked up the house phone.

"Yeah," Tony answered.

"My God! They whacked Nick! What you think we ought to do?" Eddie spoke softly, his hand covering his mouth.

"I don't know. Jesus, keep a low profile and pray," Tony said.

Alan and Suzanne

$\mathcal{A}$lan rolled over onto Suzanne's blue bedspread. He slid his arm under her pale, fine hair and pulled her head into the crook of his arm.

"Want to go to the Library for dinner tonight?" This was their evening off, and they had spent the afternoon making love.

Suzanne cuddled up to Alan's side. "Let's go someplace where they don't know you."

Alan reached for his cigarettes. He sat up and lit a Marlboro with his Zippo lighter and took a deep drag. "Why? Are you ashamed to be seen with me?"

Suzanne hugged his thigh. "No, darling, I just feel embarrassed when people look at us."

"People look at us all the time because we are a beautiful couple," Alan said, smirking. Then he turned serious. "I want to talk to you about something real important, honey." He took a deep breath, then began. "My uncle has suggested that I leave the country, go into hiding, take another identify for the rest of my life."

Suzanne sat up, her beautiful breasts spilling from beneath the white linen sheets. "You mean you'd run away?" Little frown lines appeared on her forehead.

"This is still in the suggestion stage. I guess what I want to ask is, would you go with me? There wouldn't be a problem with money. But we would have to be different people. Live different lives. You couldn't see your parents except under specially arranged circumstances. Same goes for mine." Alan looked into her eyes.

She broke eye contact. "I don't know. That's a lot to ask of a person. I'd have to think about it."

Alan put out the cigarette and pulled her into his arms. "I love you so much. I wouldn't want to live anywhere without you. If I don't do this, I'll have to go to prison for a few years. Would you wait for me until I get out? Marry a guy with a prison record?"

Suzanne pulled away and stared at him. "Marry?" That's the first time you've mentioned that. Are you proposing to me?"

"Yes, honey. I want to marry you very much. But if we leave the country, we'd have to do it under different identifies. How do you feel about that?"

"I'm not sure." Suzanne looked away.

"How would you feel about marrying me after I get out of prison?"

Suzanne shook her head. "It's too much to digest all at once. I have to think about it."

Alan pulled her chin up toward his face. "What's your gut feeling? Do you want to be with me or not?"

Her blue eyes began to tear. She hated being put on the spot. "I love you, Alan. I do want to be with you. It just seems like there are so many obstacles in our way."

He released her chin and hugged her to his chest. "Then we'll overcome them. As long as I know you want to be with me."

He laid his open mouth on hers and kissed her hard. But Suzanne felt unmoved by his passion, and when he entered her, for the first time she wasn't ready.

Ruby and Craig

Craig returned from the bank to the car where Ruby was waiting and slid behind the wheel. "All done. Now, where would you like to eat breakfast?"

"I don't care. Anywhere is okay. What happened?"

"I put the money in a safe deposit box." He showed her a small silver key.

"You keep it. I might lose it," she said.

"Do you still want a drink?" Craig asked, as he pulled into the Peppermill Restaurant parking lot.

"Not anymore. Thank God the urge is gone. Thank you so much, honey, for coming."

"That's what I'm here for, sweetie." He squeezed her thigh. "Let's have a nice leisurely breakfast, and then we'll go back to your place and tie up some loose ends."

∽

When they returned to Ruby's apartment, Craig went into Violet's room and opened her closet. Two large suitcases stood in the back. He opened them on the bed, pulled clothes from hangers, and folded them into the bags.

"What are you going to do?" Ruby asked.

"I'm going to pack all of her clothes and keep them at my place until we rent a storage locker. I'm sure someone at the club will tell the police about her involvement with Nick. When the police come, you will show Violet's note to them and tell them you haven't made arrangements yet to store her bedroom furniture. I want them to think she took all of her clothes. In a few days, I'll take you to the post office, and you'll fill out a change of address for her, like she said, care of General Delivery, Long Beach, CA." Craig scooped up the contents of the dresser drawers and dumped the clothes into the suitcases.

"What can I do?" Ruby asked.

"Why don't you go in the bathroom and remove everything that belongs to Violet and throw it away."

Ruby got a trash bag and opened the bathroom cabinet. Her things were on the first shelf and Violet's on the second. Violet's favorite scent, Chanel #5, was missing, but another perfume, Charlie, was still there, and that reminded Ruby of her. She remembered how Violet used to spray cologne on the hem of her waitress costume. She said it got her better tips. Tears brimmed over Ruby's lashes. She would probably never see her dear friend again. She felt as close to Violet as she had ever been to any woman. She dabbed at her eyes and threw several items of old makeup and mascara into the trash bag. On a shelf was a bottle of prescription Dalmane, a sleeping aid, and an envelope of amphetamines, called mini hits: small white pills. Violet would take two or three of the mini hits before going to work. Ruby threw them all in the trash. Then she tied the bag in a knot and left it in the kitchen by the garbage.

Her life had gone through so many changes lately; she wasn't always sure what to do next. One thing she knew. Her mind had become so much clearer since she'd stopped drinking. She actually liked herself these days. Her life had taken a new and positive turn. She was so fortunate to love and be loved by a good man.

Wanda, Iris and Sol

Wanda picked up the phone as she stirred a skillet of vegetables.

"Hi, it's Iris. I'm in town. Can I come over:" Her voice sounded urgent.

"Of course. Are you all right? How did you get here?" Wanda knew her sister couldn't drive.

"I took the bus. How do I get to your place?"

"Are you at the bus station downtown?" Wanda asked.

"Yes."

"Just stay there. I'll come right down and pick you up. You sure you're all right?"

"I'm okay." She didn't want to tell her sister on the phone about her bruises. Time enough for that.

Wanda turned off the stove, put the fish in the refrigerator, and left a message with Sol's message service that she was picking up Iris at the bus station.

Downtown, Wanda backed the Carmen Ghia into a convenient parking spot and walked across the street. There were several down-and-out-looking characters hanging around. One man with a bottle of Thunderbird was delivering a sermon to the sidewalk. A passersby ignored him. Just another loser in Las Vegas.

Inside the terminal, Iris was sitting in an empty row, her small bag on the floor beside her. She looked to Wanda like a small lost waif. They saw each other, and Wanda noticed immediately the bruises on Iris's face and arms.

"My God, Iris! What happened?" Even as she asked, she knew. Wanda felt sick to her stomach as she examined her sister.

"Bill."

Wanda took her sister's arm gently, picked up her bag, and directed her toward the car. "He's gone too far this time, the bastard! I'll have him arrested."

Iris began to cry. "I didn't know where to go. Naomi suggested I come here. She said she couldn't protect me, if Bill wanted me back."

"I'm glad you came, honey. You'll be safe with me. Now, don't you worry." She opened the car door for Iris, giving her an arm to lean on. Wanda slid behind the wheel and gunned the little sports car as if she were running over Big Bill.

When she pulled into her carport, she saw the Rolls in a visitor's spot. She helped Iris up the walk to her apartment.

Sol met them at the door. "I got your message and came right over." His eyes swept over Iris. "Bill do this?"

Iris nodded. She didn't trust her voice. Having two people sympathetic at the same time was more than she had ever experienced.

Wanda's eyes were dark. "The bastard beat her. He's such a coward." She escorted her sister to the couch. "Sit here, honey."

"Can I get you something to drink, Iris? Wanda?" Sol asked.

"Yes, a Coke, please," Iris answered.

"I'll have a beer," Wanda said.

Sol took a Coke and two Heinekens from the refrigerator and poured glasses for the girls. He placed the drinks on the coffee table. "Does Big Bill know you came here?"

"I didn't tell him," Iris said. "But Naomi may not be able to hold out. She always bends to his will." She took a long drink of the Coke.

"Iris, if Bill comes after you, how do you want me to handle it?" Sol asked.

Her eyes betrayed her fear. "I don't want to go back there. I can't take anymore beatings. I lost the baby." She started crying again.

Wanda, sitting beside her, put her arms around her. "Shhhh, honey. You can stay here with me. No need to go back."

Between sobs, Iris explained. "Right after you and Sol left, he beat me. I was four months pregnant. After that, he stayed sober for a couple of weeks. I think he felt bad about the baby. Then he started drinking again with his friends."

Sol spoke quietly. "I need to know how far you want me to go with Bill."

"What do you mean?" Iris asked.

"I mean, do you want Bill alive or dead?"

Iris looked shocked. "I hadn't thought about it. I

just want him discouraged from trying to get me back."

"Okay, I promise you, you don't have to go back."

Iris looked overwhelmed. "I'm so tired. I think I'll just lay down here and take a nap."

"Go in on my bed, honey." Wanda said. "If I'm gone when you wake up, don't worry. I have to go to work in a couple of hours. I'll be home around 2:30 in the morning, and I'll try not to wake you when I come in. Meanwhile, I have a roommate, Suzanne, so don't be alarmed when she walks in. She's at her boyfriends now, and she may not be home at all tonight." Wanda showed her sister the king-sized bed. "See, it's big enough for both of us." She pulled down the covers. "You just sleep as long as you need. There's food in the refrigerator when you wake up. Tomorrow I'm taking you to my doctor to make sure you're all right."

Iris grasped Wanda's hand. "Thank you."

Wanda leaned down and kissed Iris's cheek as she had done when she was a child. "We Moon girls stick together when times are rough." She left the room and shut the door quietly.

Back in the living room, Wanda said, "Listen, Sol. Please don't do anything serious. We can help Iris, but I don't want Bill's blood on my hands or yours."

He pulled her to his chest. "Don't worry, honey. I found out what Iris wants."

"We don't even know if he'll figure out she's here," Wanda said.

"I wouldn't bet on it. He'll be here. Just a matter of time."

"What will you do?"

"Don't worry yourself, my love. It will all work out okay."

Wanda hoped with all her heart that it would. For all of them.

Ruby

*R*uby heard a knock at the door. She pulled her robe around her body and opened the door to a man in a suit and tie holding up a badge. "Hi. I'm Detective Clayton from the LVPD. Is Violet Kandinsky here?"

Ruby shook her head, her uncombed curls swinging across her forehead.

"May I come in?" he said. "I'd like to ask you a few questions."

She opened the door wider and stepped back. "Excuse me, I just got up. Please come in. I'm Ruby Songer, Violet's roommate."

The policeman came in, looked around, and took a seat on the couch.

"We have a report that Miss Kandinsky hasn't showed up for work at the Calendar Club for a week. Do you know anything about this?"

Ruby swallowed. "My roommate has moved. Her aunt has cancer, and she went to take care of her. She told me she quit her job."

The policeman took out a pad and pencil. "Would you have an address where she moved?"

Ruby hesitated. "No. But I have a note she left. Would you like to read it?"

"Please," Detective Clayton said.

Ruby went to her bedroom and took the note and check from her dresser. She found herself holding her breath walking back into the living room. "She left a check for me to put her things in storage, but I haven't had a chance yet."

She handed both pieces of paper to the policeman and sat down across from him.

The detective read the note and looked at the check. He laid the check on the coffee table.

"I'd like to keep this note. May I see her room?"

"Of course." Ruby led him down the hall and opened the door. Violet's scent still hung in the room. The shades were pulled, and shadows danced across the walls as the trees outside moved against the window. Ruby flicked on the light switch.

"Thank you, Miss Songer. Would there be anything she left behind?"

She remembered that Craig hadn't emptied the desk. "You can check the desk drawers. I haven't cleaned them out yet."

Detective Clayton looked around the room. Ruby watched his eyes take in every piece of furniture, scanning all the corners, walking to the closet and sliding the door back to peer inside. His thick gray eyebrows threatened to droop over his lids. They needed trimming, Ruby thought. How could he see through them? Ruby realized she was holding here breath again. Act normal, Craig said. She inhaled shallowly so as not to attract attention.

"Thank you. I'll just be a minute." He looked pointedly at her, and Ruby got the message. She went into the kitchen and poured herself a cup of coffee. Her hand trembled as she took a sip. God, she wished Craig was here now. She sat down at the table and in a few minutes Detective Clayton came into the kitchen.

"I'm sorry," Ruby said. "I'm forgetting my manners. Would you like a cup of coffee?" She started to get up.

"No, thank you. I have to be on my way," the detective said. "I found a letter she wrote to her mother but didn't send. Do you mind if I take it now? I'll make sure it's returned along with the note."

"That's fine," Ruby said.

"Thank you for the information. By the way, did you know that Violet's boyfriend was murdered last week?" He threw the question at her suddenly.

"I…I didn't know she had a boyfriend. Who?"

The detective stared at her intensely. 'If she didn't tell you, it's not important. Here's my card. When you hear from Violet, please ask her to get in touch with me."

Ruby reached for the card with a steady hand. "Certainly, detective."

She let the policeman out and leaned against the closed door, breathing deeply now. While the detective was here it never crossed her mind to want a drink. She felt really good about herself but sad that her friendship with Violet had come to an end. She picked up the phone and called Craig.

Alan and Sol

Alan and Sol were having lunch at the Polynesian Room just off the hotel casino. Alan put down his Scotch. "I've decided, Unc. I'm going. I can't deal with jail time."

Sol wasn't surprised. "I'll start things happening. You'll need some photos for a new passport."

Alan finished his Shrimp Louie salad. "I've talked to Suzanne. She's not sure she'll go with me."

"Did you tell her it was definite?" Sol asked.

"No, not exactly. I put it to her as a possibility. I did ask her to marry me, though."

"What was her answer?"

"She didn't give me one. She said she had to think about it."

"Son, that doesn't sound too positive. By the way, what do you want your new name to be?"

"I don't care. What do you suggest?"

"I was thinking of Stein. How about Myron for a first name? Here's what I suggest. I have some property and a nice house on an island in the lower Bahamas. It's called Great Exuma. I always visit there under the name, Sol Stein. You could have a nice life as my nephew, Myron. When you need to fly to Europe, you would leave out of Nassau. We could set up meetings now and then in Europe with your parents. Meanwhile, I could visit you regularly on the island as Sol Stein. What do you think?"

Alan hung his head. "I still can't get used to it. I mean, leaving the U.S. for good."

"If you don't want to live in Great Exuma, it will be more complicated and take more money to locate you somewhere in Europe."

"No, the island sounds okay. What would I do down there?"

"There's great weather and lots of water activities. I have a sailboat, and my captain would teach you what is necessary. Lots of fishing, snorkeling and scuba. Americans and Europeans sail into Great Exuma Harbor all the time. There are a couple of decent restaurants and a golf course. "

"Yeah, Unc, but what do I do for real life?"

"Alan, you gave up the right to stay here a free man. You'll have to take potluck on the island." Sol showed his irritation in the tone of his voice. "Or…you can stay here and do your time, and then you'd be a free man, after maybe eight, ten years in prison." Sol softened his voice. "If you had Suzanne, it would definitely be more fulfilling. When you get bored, you two could go to Europe for short periods. That's the best I can offer."

Alan looked depressed. "I don't think she's gonna' go with me."

"Let me know as soon as you can. It takes time to get her passport ready. One more thing. Go to the costume shop on Maryland Parkway and buy a light mustache and a blond wig. Then, have your passport photos taken with them. Once you're relocated, you can grow a real mustache. And you need to lighten your hair. Being out in the sun bleaches hair, but yours can use some help. I want you to be ready to go in ten days. And don't do your hair until the night before you leave."

Alan looked shocked. "So soon? What do I tell the casino? I'm supposed to give a month's notice."

"I'll take care of that. I'll arrange for a substitute to do your shift when you're ready to go. Don't speak to anyone about this except Suzanne, and don't tell her details or your destination until you know she's coming."

"Guess I'll have to press her for an answer." Alan looked at his uncle with a grim face.

"You do that, son." Sol paid the bill, and they left the hotel. Sol climbed into his Rolls heading for Wanda's, and Alan drove down Maryland Parkway to a costume shop, his mind on how he could convince Suzanne to come with him.

Wanda, Suzanne, Iris and Ruby

Wanda drove along Maryland Parkway, Suzanne in the passenger seat. Iris was crunched into the back of the sports car. Iris and Suzanne seemed to like each other, and even though the apartment they all lived in was crowded with three women, Iris had endeared herself to Suzanne by keeping the place spotless, unlike Wanda's habit of leaving things scattered.

"What's going on?" Wanda asked Suzanne. "You've been so quiet the last few days. Anything wrong besides the usual?" Wanda took a left onto Desert Inn Road, heading for Ruby's.

Suzanne cast a quick glance in the back.

"Don't worry about Iris. She never talks about anything."

"Alan asked me to marry him." Suzanne stared out the window.

Wanda sneaked a peek at her. "Nice. And you're depressed about that?"

"He said we might have to get married under another name. He's thinking of leaving the country with a new identify."

Wanda knew all about that from Sol. "How do you feel about that?"

"I'm torn. I want to marry him, but I don't want to leave the country. I probably wouldn't be able to pursue my career. That's been my dream since I was a little girl." She shaded her eyes, even though they were behind sunglasses.

Wanda kept her eyes on the road. "It's probably a good bet you won't get to dance professionally if you leave with Alan. You could open a dance studio though, and teach. You wouldn't have the stress that goes with performing."

Suzanne seemed interested. "I hadn't thought of that. But I could only see my parents once a year in arranged visits in Europe. I don't think they could afford many trips abroad."

"The money can always be worked out, Suzanne. Do you love Alan?"

She turned toward Wanda. "You know I do. I just don't know if I love him enough."

Wanda realized that said it all. She pulled into the Desert Winds Apartments, parked the Carmen Ghia, and the three of them went up the outer stairs.

"You probably need to weigh both sides, then check your heart before you make a final decision," Wanda said. She knocked on the apartment door, and Ruby opened it.

"Hi, girls, come on in."

The three women entered the apartment.

"Ruby, this is my sister, Iris. She's living with us, now."

The two women exchanged hellos, and Ruby and Suzanne greeted each other.

"What are you doing in Vegas, Iris?" Ruby asked.

"I hope to open a small shop and sell Chemehuevi baskets. They're very popular in Arizona."

"Sounds like a good business," Ruby said. "Have a seat, and I'll get the costumes." She went down the hallway, returned in a few minutes with two plastic bags; one containing a Carmen Miranda costume and the second one a pareau, a long strip of material of the most brilliant red, fuchsia and turquoise colors, to be worn like a sarong.

It would look magnificent on stage, Wanda decided. Ruby had made two leis that looked like real plumeria, the flower of the islands. A tiny T-strap and G-string out of the same material completed the outfit. Wanda held the bright costume up to her. "I love it. You are so talented, Ruby."

"Thank you," she said, smiling, showing her dimples as she presented the bill. Wanda promptly wrote out a check.

"How's Violet?" Suzanne asked.

Ruby hesitated. "She's gone. She …left to take care of an aunt with cancer."

Suzanne immediately wished she hadn't asked. "I'm sorry, I didn't mean to pry."

"We heard about Nick on the news, and we hoped that Violet was all right," Wanda interceded. "She's okay?"

Ruby nodded. "She left unexpectedly. It kind of coincided with Nick's death."

"I'm glad she's okay," Wanda said. "I really liked

her, and actually, she's lucky Nick is out of her life. Of course, she probably doesn't see it that way yet."

"Probably not," Ruby said.

"Are you going to get another roommate?" Wanda asked.

"No, I'm going to move in with Craig. I can't afford the rent alone, and I don't want to live with a stranger."

"Is moving in with Craig something you want to do?" Wanda asked.

"Oh, yes, I love him. He's been so good to me and helps me stay sober. I don't know what I'd do without him."

"I'll bet you're a lot stronger than you realize," Wanda said. "You know, we women don't need a man in our lives, just because our mother's told us we did."

Iris spoke up. "That's for sure. I'm just learning that I can make it on my own."

Ruby smiled. "I'm sure you can, Iris."

Wanda took Ruby's hand. "Thank you, my dear, for your wonderful craftsmanship. Let's stay in touch. If I can help you with a ride or if you need to talk, just let me know." Wanda stepped closer and gave her a hug.

"I'm proud of you, too," Suzanne said, putting her arms around Ruby. This was very unusual for Suzanne. Wanda was the only woman she ever hugged.

"Get out of here, you guys... You're making me cry." Ruby grinned and melodramatically dabbed her eyes.

They all laughed at Ruby's comment. The three of them left and climbed into the little Carmen Ghia.

"My God! Do you think Violet had anything to do with Nick's murder?" Suzanne asked as she closed the car door.

"No, I don't think so," Wanda said. "She's running scared, obviously. I hope she makes it, and they never find her."

It was then that Suzanne realized Violet was living her life on the run.

Big Bill

Bill stepped off the Greyhound bus and walked into the terminal carrying one small bag. He smiled at the thought of Iris's face when he would appear at Wanda's apartment door. She thought she could get away, but he'd show her that she was bound to him forever. There was no escape for her. He'd drag her back to the reservation by her hair if he had to. But knowing her gentle nature, he figured she'd come back meekly enough. He planned to catch her home alone while Wanda was at work. He knew it would be easier that way. That meant he had to kill some time until evening. Maybe he'd check out the casinos downtown.

Damn Wanda! He'd always expected to have *her* for his wife. She'd been headstrong and rebellious, and he'd had the hots for her from the time she was twelve years old, throwing her body around for all to look at. Now she did it for money. He wished he'd gotten in her pants at least once before she ran away, but he could never find the right opportunity. Funny how things work out.

He went to the men's room, peed in the urinal against the wall, and walked back into the depot. He sauntered over to the candy counter, bought two Snickers bars, opened one and immediately crammed half of it into his mouth.

Outside, he saw a line of cabs and started walking

toward one. A driver down the line waved to him, so he opened the back door and slid inside. Before he could close the door, a large man with a pock-marked face jumped in beside him.

"Hey, man, this is my cab. I got here first," Big Bill insisted.

"Can't we share a cab? I'm in a real big hurry. I'll make it worth your time," the large man said.

"Yeah?" Big Bill looked interested. "How will you make it worth my time?"

"1620 Las Vegas Blvd," Ace Brooks said to the driver. He pulled a small caliber handgun from his inside pocket and stuck it in Bill's ribs. "Why, I thought I'd give you a free ride back to Parker."

Bill was shocked at the gun. "How'd you know I'm from Parker?"

"Oh, a little bird told me," Ace said.

"What if I was to say you got the wrong man. I'm not from Parker."

Ace pulled a small photo of Big Bill from his breast pocket. "Then I'd say you were a liar." He held up the picture.

Bill's face paled. "What do you want with me?"

"I want to know what your business is here."

"Well…uh, I came up to see my wife. She's staying with her sister."

"And who might your wife be?"

"Iris. Iris Blueknife. We're Native Americans, in case you didn't know."

"Oh yeah? Say, pal, what if your wife don't want to see you?"

"How would you know that?"

"I know, believe me."

The cab driver stopped at the address on Las Vegas Blvd. A neon sign flashed GOLD'S JEWELRY over the entrance.

"We're getting out here. Thanks, Russ," Ace said to the cab driver as he shoved Bill out the door, holding the gun against the Indian's back in a concealed manner.

"Sure thing," Russ said, and drove off.

"Hey, where are you taking me?" Bill was forced to walk in front of Ace.

"We're going down this alley and in the back door. You just do as I say."

They entered the back of the jewelry shop and went down a hallway. Bill's hands were shaking, and his gray tee shirt revealed wet stains under the armpits. Ace opened a door and pushed Bill into a dark room. "I'll be back, you can be sure of that."

Bill heard the door lock. He immediately went to the window and saw that it was boarded up from the outside. In the dim light filtering through the slats across the window he could see boxes haphazardly stacked against the walls. A thin mattress and a dirty blanket lay on the floor in one corner. A plastic bowl held some water, and a rusty pail rested beside the mattress. He heard scratching noises among the boxes and thought he saw one move slightly. Bill hadn't faced fear in a long time, but he suddenly felt the taste of it in the back of his throat. A sharp stinging sensation threatened to cut off his air. It tasted a lot like the time he almost drowned in the Colorado River when he was a kid.

Wanda and Sol

Wanda blew out the candle beside the bed and snuggled down into Sol's hard arms. He kissed her on the temple. "Baby, you're the best thing that ever happened to me. How'd you like to go on a trip? A long trip."

"Where?" Wanda murmured sleepily.

"I was thinking it's time we took a trip around the world. We'd start out in Tahiti. I have some friends there with a place on one of the smaller islands. Then when we get tired of the lazy, sun-drenched days and tropical nights," Sol squeezed Wanda, "we can fly to Singapore and hang out with a Chinese friend of mine. Then from there, we could go to Hong Kong, Bangkok or head for the Seychelles."

Wand cocked her head to look up at Sol. "My God! You're really serious. It would take a long time to do that."

"That's the idea." Sol kissed her gently.

"You know I have to work. I have a contract with Richie. I don't have the money to quit and just take off."

"That was my other question. I was wondering if you would do me the honor of marrying me."

Wanda sat up, wide awake now, the satin sheet falling away from her brown breasts. She looked at Sol as a tear slide down her cheek.

He wiped it away with his thumb. "Well?"

"Oh, yes, darling. I'd love to be your wife."

"Then it's settled. When shall we have the wedding? Do you want a big one with your family, or a small one?"

"No, not my family. I can't deal with that. What about you? Do you have any family besides Alan? You've never said."

Sol pulled her back down under the covers. "None out here. Alan's dad is my brother, lives back in Bloomfield Hills, Michigan. Alan will probably be gone in a few days. Shall we elope?"

"Yes, that sounds wonderful!"

"I've never been married before," Sol confided. "I just never wanted anyone forever, until you."

Wanda wound her legs around his. "I've never been married, either. We're first timers, darling. That's good luck here in Vegas."

"We could book passage to Tahiti," Sol said, "and get married by the captain on the high seas."

"That sounds very romantic. I like that idea. But first I have to get Iris settled. She wants to look for a place where she can sell her baskets, but she's still afraid Bill will come looking for her."

Sol put one arm behind his head and cuddled Wanda with the other. "I wouldn't worry about Bill. He's recuperating in Parker hospital. Seems he got hit by a car and broke both his legs."

Wanda looked up, horrified. "Sol. What really happened?"

"Sweetheart, just be confident that he won't bother Iris ever again. She can get a divorce up here when she's ready. Big Bill will stay down there, I guarantee it."

Thank God, Iris would be safe. Wanda wondered if Iris could assimilate as easily as she had. She knew that was what she really wanted for her little sister.

Suzanne and Alan

Suzanne and Alan were eating at Gus Gallo's out on Paradise Road. Since Gus served the best Italian food in the city and was sometimes frequented by the more mysterious elements of Las Vegas, Alan guessed Suzanne would be less likely to be stared at here.

He stubbed out a cigarette and drained his Scotch. He figured it was now or never and took a long, deep breath. "I'm going to leave the U.S. in five days. Will you go with me?"

Suzanne's martini glass froze on its way to her mouth. "You've decided?"

Alan nodded. He beckoned the waiter for another Scotch. "Want another?"

She shook her head. "Why so soon?"

He saw the pain in her face. "I need to go as soon as possible. Sol has everything arranged, except your passport. He can do that in a couple of days."

"Where are you going?" She asked, sipping her drink.

"I'm going to a small tropical island where Sol has a place. I'm hoping *we* are going there."

She ignored his comment. "What will be your new name?"

"Myron Stein. It's a cover that Sol had set up for himself years ago, in case he needed it. Now, he's giving it to me."

The waiter brought steaming plates of Three Cheese Ravioli with Marinara Sauce, and set another Scotch before Alan.

Suzanne picked at her food. "I don't understand why you have to go so soon. Your court date isn't for another two months."

"Because Sol said most people run near their court appearances. He thinks I should go now, when it's least expected."

"What about your job and your house?"

"Sol will take care of all that. I'm going to be a fugitive for the rest of my life. But there will be money for us. We won't want for anything." He took her hand across the table.

She continued to avoid his eyes, rolling a ravioli around her plate.

Looking up, she said, "You're growing a mustache."

"Yes, in a few days my hair will be blond. Do you like blonds, love?" He continued to hold her hand.

Finally, she pulled away. "I guess so. Hair isn't what's important."

"What is important, Suzanne?" Alan's voice sounded harsh.

"Marriage and children. Being able to take the kids home to their grandparents. Going to PTA meetings. Teaching a dance class." A tear rolled down her cheek.

"Well, fuck! That's not the kind of life I can offer you. If you wanted that life, why the fuck did you ever become a dancer? I never would have guessed that the

PTA was important to you."

Her shoulders began to shake. "Excuse me," she said and stood up abruptly, her napkin falling to the floor. She left the dining room hurriedly and went to the ladies' room. She stumbled into a stall and leaned against the door and wept.

Alan paid the check and was having a third Scotch when she returned. A small glass of port rested at her place. She sat down and sipped it. Her eyes were red, and he could see a fresh layer of powder across her cheeks.

"I guess I don't have to ask, but I'm going to, anyway. I want to hear it from your lips. Are you coming with me?"

Suzanne pressed her lips together and tried to utter a word. Finally, she shook her head, her lovely blue eyes again full of tears.

Alan hung his head. "Why not?"

She was able to speak now. "Darling, I wouldn't be any good for you. I would hate our life, eventually. I might even make a mistake, and they would catch us."

"I won't let you make a mistake," he said fiercely. "I want you with me."

Suzanne was silent, her face still wet.

He looked at her for several seconds, searching her eyes, trying to understand this woman he loved. Then he stood, picked up her shawl, placed it around her shoulders, and they walked single file from the restaurant.

Ruby

Ruby's head swam as she lowered the box onto Craig's bed. What the hell could be wrong, she thought? Ever since she'd stopped drinking, she had enjoyed extremely good health. Feeling suddenly queasy, she dashed to the bathroom, placed her head over the toilet and threw up her breakfast. Puzzled, she wiped her mouth and face with a wet cloth, brushing tousled curls away from her eyes. She hadn't had a drink in months, so why would she throw up? Her hand slowly moved down to her belly. An awakening flowed over her like a new day.

Craig came in and threw some clothes on the bed, glancing at her face. "What's wrong, honey?"

"I think I'm pregnant." Ruby smiled.

Craig was speechless. He searched her eyes to see if she was joking and decided she wasn't.

"What makes you think that?"

"I've been sick to my stomach all morning, and I just threw up. I've been kind of nauseous the last few days."

Craig sat down on the end of the bed. Clothes and hangers slipped unnoticed to the floor. "Well, that puts a different spin on things. I think you'd better visit your doctor real soon." He gazed past her in deep thought.

"I'll make an appointment this afternoon." She looked up at him. "Do you want a baby, Craig?"

His eyes moved to her face. "Hell, yes, I want *our* baby. How about you?"

"I've always thought I couldn't have kids. I've never been pregnant before. I'd love to have a child."

He reached over and pulled her into his arms. "If you are, we need to leave this town soon. We don't want our baby born here."

Ruby looked at him and nodded. "Yes, you're right. But where? And what would we do?"

"We'll figure it out, don't worry. I can always drive a cab, and you can design and sew clothes better than Bob Mackie. We'll be just fine. And, we can also start using the money, once we leave here."

"Oh, you think we dare?"

"You bet. We'll be safe once we're out of this town. We won't spend a lot of money. Maybe just enough for a little house in the country." Craig took her left hand in his. "Baby, will you marry me?"

Ruby gasped. "Oh, Craig, yes!"

"I was going to ask you anyway, once you were moved in." He kissed her.

"You were? I never thought that you would, I mean...ask me to marry you." Her eyes shone with moisture.

"I wanted to ask you months ago. Waiting for you to get sober was worth it."

Ruby stood up. "I'm so happy, Craig. My head's spinning with plans and all kinds of questions." She picked up the clothes from the rug.

"Now, honey," Craig said, pushing her gently back on the bed. "You take it easy. No more lifting boxes. I'll unload the car. You lie down and rest for a while." He rushed out of the apartment, eager to finish the work.

Ruby relaxed against the soft pillows with her eyes closed, hands caressing her flat belly. Would it be a boy or a girl? Would she have an easy time delivering? One thing was for damn sure. She would make life a lot easier for their child than it had been for her. She would watch over him or her with fierce mother love. And no one better dare take advantage of her child.

Iris, Wanda and Sol

Sol parked the Rolls in front of a store with a flashing neon sign that read GOLD'S JEWELRY.

He stepped out and opened the back door for Iris and Wanda. Iris wasn't used to this gentlemanly behavior and didn't know whether she liked it or not when he walked ahead and held open the glass door of the store for them. At the back, a large man with curly gray hair and a cigar in his mouth sat at a desk.

"Hi, Manny. My fiancée, Wanda Moon, and her sister, Iris Blueknife." Sol put his arm round Wanda.

Manny stood and moved the cigar to the other side of his mouth. "Nice to meet ya' ladies. Glad you could come by today. I'm clearing out a counter in front," he said, waving toward the big glass windows. He turned to Iris. "When you wanna' start?"

Everyone turned to look at her.

She took a deep breath. "I'll have a first shipment this week. My brother is bringing a load up here."

"Fine," Manny said. "You can come in any time and get set up. I guess Sol told you I'll take twenty percent of what you make."

Iris nodded.

"In case you didn't know," Sol directed his remarks to Manny, "Chemehuevi baskets are considered prized pieces of art these days. So when you advertise, keep that in mind. You might help Iris price them, as they'll go for even more in Vegas. And one other thing, Manny, if there are any problems regarding Iris or her business, I've left instructions with Irv, my attorney. He has the authority to straighten them out. I expect you to look after her when she's here. Understood?"

Manny and Sol exchanged looks. "Completely understood, Sol. I'll take good care of her. Irv's my lawyer too, ya' know."

"That's right, I'd forgotten," Sol said. "I don't want Iris going home on the bus. You put her in a cab every night."

"Right, Sol. I'll see to it." Manny smiled at Wanda. "So, you and Sol are going on a cruise to Tahiti? Fantastic! When are ya' leavin?"

"Next week," Sol replied. "We're getting married on board ship."

"Congratulations to both of you, and have a wonderful trip." He turned to Iris. "May I call you Iris?"

"Of course. May I call you Mr. Gold?"

"Manny will be fine. If we're gonna' work together, we might as well be on a first name basis."

"Thanks, Manny," Wanda said, "for giving Iris this opportunity."

"Absolutely, happy to be of help." Manny smiled at both women.

Sol offered his hand. "Thanks, again." He turned to Wanda. "Why don't you and Iris go get in the car, I'll be out in a minute. I need to leave some phone numbers with Manny."

When the front door chimed on the women's exit, Sol took an envelope from his breast pocket. "This ought to carry you through until I get back. If you need any more funds, just call Irv. There should be plenty here to take care of Iris's expenses and some for you, too."

Manny took the envelope, and without opening it, stuck it in a desk drawer. "Don't worry about your future sister-in-law. Between Irv and me, we'll make sure she's fine, and of course there's always Ace if her no-good husband comes around."

"Thanks, a million, Manny."

"Bon voyage, my friend." Manny waved as Sol went out the front door.

Alan

$\mathcal{A}$ tall blond man in his thirties with a light brown mustache stepped up to the United Airlines counter.

"Here are your tickets, Mr. Stein. Your connecting flight will leave Miami an hour after you land. Have a good trip." The airlines person handed him the first-class ticket and smiled.

Alan immediately went to the bar and ordered a double Scotch. Sol couldn't come to the airport to see him off because someone might recognize them. No uncle and no Suzanne. That was the heartbreaker. He'd fucked up his life royally. He knew he would see his Uncle Sol occasionally on his island refuge, but to never see or hold Suzanne again was almost more than he could stand. The thought of living without her had often reduced him to tears.

Their last night together after they had eaten at Gus Gallo's restaurant had been less than satisfying. She had been uptight and hadn't responded to his lovemaking. It was all he could do to finish, after holding back for her. When he finally came, he only felt sorrow. He took her home and begged her to change her mind. She continued to stand her ground, sliding from the car with tears running down her face. She ran up the stairs and turned once to look back at him. Then she entered her apartment and swiftly closed the door.

Alan didn't look forward to a life of tropical sun and solitude. He'd grown accustomed to Las Vegas, its exciting night life, the cadence of the casinos. That part he would sorely miss.

He ordered another double from the airport bar, hoping the alcohol would deaden his pain. She had flat out rejected him. Yesterday she would not take or return his calls. She never could have really loved him. However, beneath his self-pity he knew in his heart that Suzanne had loved him. As much as she was capable of…just not enough.

"Flight 401 for Miami, boarding at Gate 10." He heard the announcement over the PA system. He chugged the last of his Scotch, picked up his one suitcase, and walked steadily to the gate. He boarded the plane and found his seat beside the window. In a few minutes the stewardess brought him a Scotch. He might as well get loaded while the plane did the same.

When the 747 lifted off the tarmac, Alan took a last look at his home country, the United States of America. He gazed down at the sea of swimming pools, like little emerald jewels glittering in the morning sun. The twenty-four-hour lights of the Strip cut a swath through the town. To the left, beyond the city, Sunrise Mountain rose above the gambling mecca. On the other side of the valley, Mount Charleston stood in guarded repose over the Vegas basin. Tears sprang to his eyes. He could never come home again.

Sol and Wanda

Wanda and Sol had a leisurely breakfast in bed at his penthouse. Throwing the covers back, she slipped her legs over the side. Standing in the pink negligee he had given her, she stretched her long arms above her head and then, bending at the waist, touched her toes.

Sol came out of the bathroom with his tie hanging around his neck. "Sweetheart, will you tie this damn thing? I'm going to rip it to pieces if it doesn't start cooperating."

Wanda laughed as she skillfully tied it and tugged down his collar.

"I have to go to the personnel department this morning and arrange for a dealer to cover Alan's shift tonight."

"I'm going home to be with Suzanne," Wanda said, returning to her stretching exercises.

"I expect she'll be feeling pretty low about now," Sol said. "She'll welcome your company. I'm sure sorry she didn't go with Alan."

"In a way, so am I. But you know, she wants to continue her dancing career. I understand that."

"She could have had the man she loved and a rich, leisurely life," Sol said. "I'll never understand how she preferred a career."

Wanda walked to the long windows covered by a transparent silk curtain. "I might want to return to the

Arabesque Club sometime." She turned toward him. "Would that be all right with you?"

Sol dropped his eyes and started looking around the bedroom. "We have months yet before we'll be back in Vegas. There's lots of time to decide. Besides, you haven't even quit yet."

She walked up to him and slipped her arms around his waist. "Sol, I need to know now. Will you respect my need to continue dancing if I want to?"

He embraced her. "Sweetheart, you don't need to work. I have enough money to last us all our lives."

"I know, but it's your money," she said. "I want to have my own money. Besides, it's not really the money. I want to perform. I guess I have a need for a certain amount of adulation."

Sol looked down at her. "Wanda, when we're married, I don't want my wife being leered at by every man in Vegas. And I'll give you all the adulation you want. I'll set up your own checking account. It will be your money."

Wanda stepped back. "You never complained about my profession before. It was okay with you while you were courting me."

"We can discuss this later, honey. It's not something we have to decide today."

Wanda insisted, "Yes, it is. It's something we must settle before we get married."

She stared at him intensely.

Sol shook his head. "Sweetheart, you're asking too

much. I can take you out of that world. As my wife you can have any damn thing you want."

"I don't want you to take me out of *that world*. I like what I do. Don't you understand that?"

He ran his fingers through his hair and looked at his watch. "Please, let's continue this discussion tonight. I have to go." He walked to the dresser and picked up his wallet and keys. "Shall I pick you up tonight at the club?"

Wanda shook her head and replied in a cool manner, "No. I'll drive to work. You can come over when I get home." she added, "if you want."

"Don't you want to spend the night here with me?"

"No, I want you to spend the night at my place with me."

Sol sighed deeply. "Okay. I'll be there around 3 a.m." He hated to walk around Iris sleeping on the couch, but instinct told him to humor Wanda right now.

He left without kissing her. He had never gone before without an embrace. She didn't want to lose him, but she also had to have her independence in deciding her own future. Was Sol going to be like every man she had ever cared about? Not able to accept her for who she was?

Sol

Sol steered his silver Rolls Royce out of the underground garage as he chewed a hangnail on his thumb. What the hell was happening with Wanda? He figured she'd want to spend the rest of her life with him, no longer needing to be on the stage. He'd take her out of her old life and give her a new one. That had been his plan. Apparently, he needed to revise it. He loved Wanda very much, and he wasn't about to lose her, but he had to convince her that he couldn't keep his respect and stature with his peers if his wife stripped for a living.

He turned into the circular drive at the entrance to the El Morocco Hotel and Casino. Jimmy, the valet, opened his door.

"Park this car somewhere safe, Jimmy," Sol said as he handed him a fifty.

"Yes sir, Mr. Wolfe, I'll take good care of it. Thank you," he said as he identified the bill.

Sol entered the hotel and took the elevator to the eleventh floor. He walked into the Director of Personnel's office, Art Cassio.

"Hi, Art. How's it going?" Sol asked as he perched his rear on Art's desk.

"Great, Sol. How about you?"

"I'm fine. How's the family?"

"Good. Billy, my oldest, is graduating soon, and my youngest, Eric, is doing great in fifth grade."

"How's your wife?"

"Good, Sol. Thanks for asking. What's up?"

"My nephew, Alan Wolfe, has left town on urgent business, and I need you to replace him on the schedule."

Art paused. "Sure, no problem. How long will he be gone?"

"A long time," Sol replied.

"Okay." Art's friendly expression never changed. "I've got a couple of people on standby. I'll put one of them to work."

"You need to cover his shift tonight."

"Sure thing."

"One more thing, Art. Don't mention Alan's leaving to anyone yet."

"Understood, Sol." Art nodded and smiled. "By the way, one of our regular high rollers asked for Suzanne Cane last night. Want to put her back on the party list?"

Sol stared out the window. "No, leave her off permanently." He stood and offered his hand. "Thanks, Art. See you." Sol left and headed for the elevator.

Art watched him through the glass window of his office. He saw a handsome, confident man, completely at ease in his environment, who always got everything he wanted. A powerful man. God, how he envied him! He wished he had his money and savoir faire. He also knew instinctively never to cross or displease Sol Wolfe. That would be a severe mistake.

He knew about Alan's problems with the law and figured he was gone for good. Suzanne Cane now was something else. Maybe Sol reserved her for himself. Who knows? But he'd keep his mouth shut and his family, job and his life safe.

Wanda and Suzanne

*I*t was early afternoon when Wanda entered her apartment. Suzanne was in the kitchen, making coffee. She looked up with red-rimmed eyes and pink nose.

"What's happening, honey?" Wanda knew but wanted to give her a chance to talk.

"Alan's gone. His plane left two hours ago," she sobbed. "I'll never see him again."

Wanda went over and put her arms around her. Suzanne cried on her shoulder, her body shaking.

"Honey, I'm sorry. Here, sit down. I'll pour you some coffee. Want some breakfast?"

Suzanne shook her head and sat at the kitchen table, twisting a damp tissue. Finally she blew her nose.

"Things seem really black right now," Wanda said. "But you know, you made your own decision. I admire you for that. Not letting anyone push you into something you didn't want." Wanda put the cup in front of her.

"You do?" Suzanne took a sip of the freshly poured coffee.

"Yes, dear, I do. I know how much a career in dancing means to you. At the same time, I know you love Alan."

Suzanne nodded. "I do love him. But I know in my heart that I would grow to hate him in that kind of life."

The two women sat silently drinking coffee. Wanda felt a lump in her throat. She didn't know if she and Sol had a future together after this morning. She couldn't marry him on his terms. Being independent was too important to her.

"Are you going to stay with the show for awhile?" Wanda asked.

"I guess so, until something better comes along. I was thinking of auditioning for a show on the road."

"That sounds like a good idea. They're always looking for new talent. One of the strippers down at the Arabesque got a job in the chorus with a show going to Haiti."

Suzanne nodded again. "Yes, I think I'd like that. I need more experience on my resume in case I decide to go to New York."

"Anything I can do to help, honey, just let me know."

Suzanne wiped her nose. "Thanks, Wanda. I don't know what I'd so without your friendship and advice."

"Why don't we do some serious shopping tomorrow at Saks and I. Magnin," Wanda suggested. "Sound good?" She put her arm around Suzanne's shoulder. Wanda felt she needed a little distraction, too.

"Yes, that sounds like fun. Just the two of us." For the first time, Suzanne smiled.

Wanda pulled ice cubes from the refrigerator and fixed a cold pack in a towel. "Now put this on your swollen eyes. It's almost showtime, girl!"

Ruby and Craig

*R*uby opened the door of the cab and hopped inside. She looked at Craig with large, teary eyes and a big smile. "We're going to have a baby!"

Craig leaned over and kissed her on the lips. "Great! How far along are you?"

"The doctor says fourteen weeks."

"How you feeling?" Craig asked.

"I feel good. He says this morning sickness should pass pretty soon." When her stomach was calm, Ruby hadn't felt this good in a long time. She had quit smoking as soon as she suspected she might be pregnant, mostly because it made her nauseous, but also because instinctively she knew it was bad for the baby.

Craig slid his tanned arm along the back of the seat, caressing her neck, and stared thoughtfully across Maryland Parkway. "Ruby, I think it's time to leave. Right away. That okay with you?"

"What's our hurry, honey?"

"I'm thinking about our safety and our baby's. That detective never got back in touch with you, but I'm betting he will eventually. It won't be very hard for him to find out you're living with me. I don't want any questions to come up that we can't answer." Craig backed out of the professional building's parking lot and headed home.

"I have a couple of costumes to finish for a friend of Wanda's. I can get that done in the next few days and then start packing."

"Good," Craig replied. "We'll rent a U-haul and tow it behind the cab. That should hold all our furniture. Where shall we go, sweetheart?" Ruby had thought about it a lot and hadn't come to any decisions. She shook her head. "Gee, I don't know."

"We're gonna' disappear. We're not gonna tell anyone where we're going." He glanced over at Ruby. "It's important that we cut all ties with Vegas. That means Wanda, too. Think you can do that?"

Ruby nodded. The only person she would want to tell is Wanda. But she thought her friend would understand.

Craig turned into his parking space at the apartment. "We could go north to Reno, or south to Arizona, or into New Mexico." Craig was daydreaming aloud. "We'll get married in our new town. And you'll have a new name. We'll start a new life, along with that new little life in your belly." He laid his hand gently on Ruby's stomach. "I love you, Ruby. I'm so proud of you."

He pulled her into his arms.

Wanda

*F*rom the wings Wanda watched the woman on stage skillfully remove her sequined dress, then the rhinestone-studded bra and T-strap, all in the old style of burlesque, slowly, tantalizing, constantly draping her feather boa across her bosom so the audience could only see her gleaming shoulders, arms and long legs clad in black stockings. Just before the lights dimmed, her final move was to lower the boa and reveal her large white breasts. The audience clapped, cheered and stomped their feet as Magnolia Blossom exited the stage.

The seasoned performer walked to her dressing room in the back of the building. Magnolia had begun her career in the days when there was a burlesque house or two in every big city. Still beautiful and still stripping, Magnolia came to the Arabesque Club in Vegas once a year, as she made the rounds on the U.S, and Canadian circuit.

Wanda followed her down the hallway and knocked at the silver door with the sparkling star.

"Yes, who is it?" Magnolia's musical voice asked.

"Wanda."

"Come on in, honey," she said, her southern drawl apparent.

When Wanda entered, Magnolia was seated at the dressing table, removing the wig of strawberry curls. Her natural hair was the color of pebbles on a river bottom. She wiped her forehead with a tissue.

"Sit down, Wanda." She stood up and wrapped a silk kimono around her curvaceous body. Skin white as milk, her face had few lines, character lines Sol would call them. For an old-timer, she was remarkably youthful. The way her breasts stood upright, Wanda figured she'd had a few tucks to keep them there.

"I want to chat with you for a minute, Maggie. Do you mind?" Wanda seated herself on the chaise lounge.

"Sure thing, honey. What's up?"

Wanda had known Magnolia for six years but not really well. Their contact was at the club, except for a few times they'd had dinner together, talking mostly about show business.

"I'm thinking of getting married. I guess I just want to get your perspective. You ever been married?"

Magnolia cast large blue eyes at Wanda. "Several times, darlin'. I married my first manager first. Thought it would be okay, since we traveled together. Well, when I realized that I never had a dime in the bank, I knew he was robbing me of my money, so I dumped him. Next manager I made the mistake of marryin' too. He drank up the money. Let's see, there was a cowboy in there somewhere and a travelin' salesman. I couldn't afford to quit work, seemed like I was always supportin' a husband." She smirked at Wanda in the mirror, inserted a cigarette into her tortoise-shell holder and lit it. She inhaled deeply and blew smoke rings into the mirror. "So honey, you think you might wanna' hang up your G-string?"

"Sol wants me to. He says he doesn't want other men leering at me."

"He sounds like a good man to have for a husband. Who is he?"

"Sol Wolfe, part owner of the El Morocco."

"Oh, *that* Sol. I understand why he feels that way. He doesn't want his business acquaintances to think he's controlled by a woman who strips for a living. It's awful hard to find a good man, ever, in this world. When we do, hang on to him. If any of mine had wanted me to quit strippin', why I'd have traded my G-string for an apron quicker than biscuits rise!"

"You wouldn't have missed the applause?"

"Hell, no. If the truth be known, I'm pretty tired of it after forty years." Magnolia crossed one shapely calf over a bare thigh. "Course, we're all different, but if you was to ask me for advice…" she paused dramatically, pulling on her cigarette, "well, I just gave it to you."

"Thanks, Maggie. I really appreciate you sharing experiences. You know, I wouldn't talk about anything you said to me." Wanda stood.

"I know that, honey, else I wouldn't be talkin' to you."

"I got to get ready for my next set. See you later." Wanda put her hand on Magnolia's shoulder. "By the way, you really knocked 'em dead, out there. Wish I could strip with the class that you have."

"Wanda, you're a dancer, I never was. You do just fine." Magnolia patted Wanda's buns. "Just remember, all the guys in the world puttin' their palms together can't equal love with that special man."

"Thanks, Maggie." She left the dressing room and headed back to the community room.

Brady and Iris

*I*ris opened the apartment door and found Brady slouched on the porch.

"Hi, Sis," he said, as he stepped inside and gave her a bear hug.

Iris returned his hug, then pulled back and looked at her brother. "You look good. Been taking care of yerself, I see."

"Yep, I've been a good boy. Stayin' out of trouble." He gave her a big smile, showing perfect teeth. "My car's loaded with baskets. What you want me to do with 'em?"

"We'll take them down to the store after awhile. Come in. Want some coffee? Something to eat?"

Brady shut the door. "I can always eat, Sis." He gazed around the apartment. "Nice place here. You and Wanda did okay." Admiring the fresh carnations standing in a vase on the table, he realized it was a woman's touch that made the apartment so appealing.

"Suzanne lives here too," Iris said. "She's Wanda's roommate. You'll meet her later. This is hers and Wanda's taste, not mine."

"What's the matter, you don't like these digs?" He took a chair at the table while Iris poured two cups of coffee and placed a chocolate doughnut in front of him.

"Sure, I like it fine. It's just not what I do with it if it were mine. But I'm real grateful for Wanda taking me in."

Brady studied his sister for a moment, then decided she was fine.

"How are Naomi and Jackson?" Iris asked.

"They're doing good. Sent their love. Naomi sent a bunch of fry bread and canned corn. Guess she thinks you don't get enough to eat up here." He smiled at his sister. "Wanna' know about Bill?"

"No, I really don't care as long as he leaves me alone." But Iris fell silent as if waiting to hear the news her brother might tell.

Brady licked the last crumbs from the plate. "One of his broken legs didn't heal real good. He limps on it and still has a cast on the other. But he's working as a night watchman at one of the grain silos on the reservation. At least he's drawin' a salary. And he hasn't been drinkin' much."

Iris' expression remained inscrutable as she thought of the lonely nights. But she counted her blessings that he would never be close enough to strike her again. "Did they ever catch the driver that hit him?" she asked.

"Nope. Hit and run. No witnesses and Bill was too drunk to remember anything. So what's happening in Vegas for you, Sis? And how's Wanda?" He finished his coffee and put the cup in the sink.

"I told you I was gonna' sell baskets out of the front of a jewelry store. Sol was kind enough to arrange everything with the owner, who's a friend of his." She took a deep breath and continued. "As for Wanda, she and Sol are getting married."

Brady whistled. "Our sister is doing all right for herself. Figure the way he spent money to keep me out of jail, he's pretty loaded."

"Sol's a good man, and he loves Wanda a lot," Iris said, firmly. "He has a lot of influence in this town, and it would be a mistake not to treat him with respect."

"Yeah, I get it, Sis, Far be it from me to mess anything up. So our big sister's gonna' marry a white man. Does Naomi know?"

"I don't think Wanda has told her yet, it all happened so fast."

"Is she gonna' continue to take her clothes off, on stage, I mean, after she's married?"

"I don't know. Wanda hasn't said. But I don't think Sol likes it, and I'm betting she'll quit her job."

Brady nodded, tipping back in his chair, balancing on the back legs. "If he's half the man you say he is, he won't let her dance bare-ass anymore. But I think Wanda will resist. Our sister's an extremely headstrong, independent woman."

Iris nodded. "Yes, but Wanda's in love. She isn't going to mess up her life and risk losing Sol."

"We'll see," Brady said, gazing off into space.

Suzanne

Suzanne hung up her costume, took off her stage makeup and dressed in her white slacks and pink tank top. She slammed her locker door, and twirled the combination.

One of the showgirls, a lovely redhead, watched her leave. "Suzanne, how come you don't come to the after-hour parties anymore?"

Suzanne turned. "I, uh, don't get invited anymore. That's fine with me."

"I'm going upstairs to a party right now. Wanna' come?" The redhead arched her left eyebrow.

"No, thanks. I have another appointment." Suzanne turned and headed out of the dressing room and the casino. She had no appointment, but upstairs was the last place she wanted to go. She felt restless. Alan had been gone a week and she'd cried herself to sleep every night since he'd left. A cloud of cigarette smoke hung along the high ceiling of the casino, causing Suzanne to sneeze and cough as she passed through the slot area. She walked out the front entrance, crossed the street at the light, and headed into the Dunes. An employee could not gamble in the club in which they worked. This was a rule in every casino. She entered the Dunes, and turned toward the slots. She changed a twenty, perched on a red stool and began dumping quarters, three at a time, into the machine. After twenty minutes and receiving only a few quarters back, she'd used up the money. Signaling the change girl, she bought another roll of quarters. Suzanne continued to gamble, having no idea how much money she fed into the hungry machine or how much time passed. A calming numbness overtook her. For the first time in days, she didn't think of Alan. In fact, she thought of nothing. Her hand moved up and down, from paper cup to slot, almost as if she were directing traffic. When she reached into her purse and found she had no more paper money in her wallet, she got off the stool and headed back across the street to her car. Glancing at her watch, she saw it was 5 a.m. She stifled a yawn, unlocked the car door, and headed home. When she laid her head on the pillow her eyes were dry, and she knew she would sleep.

Ruby and Craig

Craig stuffed the last box into the U-haul van and closed the back doors. He walked back to the second-floor apartment that he and Ruby had shared for two weeks. Admiring Ruby's rounded backside as she vacuumed the rug, he finished cleaning the bathroom, tossing the empty Comet can into the trash bag. Ruby was bent over winding the vacuum cord, and he patted her bottom gently.

"That's it, babe. We're finished here. Let's hit the road." He picked up the vacuum with his free hand. "Lock the door, and we'll drop off the keys at the office."

He placed the machine in the back seat and slid behind the wheel. When Ruby got comfortable in the passenger side, he headed for the office. Craig got out of the cab and pushed the keys into the slot of the office door. When he returned, he noticed an unmarked police car pull up behind the building. Craig drove behind the line of carports and parked. He nudged Ruby and pointed to the detective getting out of the police car and walking up to their second-floor apartment. They saw him knock on the door; he was holding papers in his hand. The detective knocked several times, then came down the stairs and headed for the office. Craig and Ruby' car was hidden so the detective could not see them. He knocked at the office door and saw the sign that said they were out to lunch.

"Oh, Craig, let's go, get out of here, please!" There was fear in Ruby's voice.

"We need to stay here until he leaves," Craig said quietly.

Presently the policeman walked to his unmarked car, got in and headed out of the parking lot away from where Craig and Ruby were parked.

When his car disappeared from view, Craig drove away in the opposite direction. They headed for the freeway.

"I wish I could have called Wanda. She'll wonder what happened to me." Ruby stared out the window as they passed the high-rise hotels on the Strip.

"Wanda knows you're okay now. You're with me." Craig said. Keeping his eyes on the road he took Ruby's hand in his.

"I know, but she was the only friend I had, except for Violet," Ruby said wistfully.

"Honey, you'll make new friends. I know you will. And you have me. I'm your friend."

Ruby squeezed his hand. "I know you are. Forgive me for feeling sorry for myself. Of course you're right. I'm truly blessed, and I know that."

"We both are. We're on our way, honey, to a new life."

Earlier that morning he'd gone to the bank and cleaned out the safe deposit box, stashing the cash beneath the trunk floor. He drove onto the freeway passing under the sign that read RENO.

Wanda, Iris, Suzanne and Brady

Wanda entered the apartment and saw her brother sitting on the couch. Iris was cooking in the kitchen.

This was Brady's second trip to Vegas to bring the Chemehuevi baskets for Iris's business. He hadn't seen Wanda the first time he came, a few weeks earlier. He gave her a big hug. "Hi, Sis. How you doin'?"

"Fine, how about you, little brother?" She scanned him from head to toe. His dark complexion and blue-black hair were nature's gifts, and he wore them handsomely.

"You're looking well."

"Yeah. I'm doing okay." Brady said dropping his arm from her waist as they walked into the kitchen.

"Did you have enough room for all the baskets at the store?" Wanda asked her sister.

"Manny let me put some of them in a vacant room in back. And I made a display in the front window."

Wanda pulled two bottles of beer from the refrigerator, opened them, and handed one to Brady. "You want anything, Iris?"

"Some ice tea, please." Iris never drank alcohol, maybe because Big Bill did.

Wanda poured the tea and set it within Iris's reach. "So have you sold many baskets?" she asked.

"Quite a few," Iris replied. "I think all Manny's friends' wives have been in to buy them."

Wanda laughed. "Guess that's his way of taking

care of you. Don't worry. Pretty soon the word will get around, and strangers will be coming in." Wanda sniffed the air. "Something smells good. What's for dinner?"

"Fried chicken, mashed potatoes, gravy and creamed corn and fry bread from Naomi," Iris answered.

Wanda was getting pretty tired of canned corn and fry bread, and Iris leaned heavily on fried foods, too. Since her sister's arrival, Wanda had put on a few pounds. She needed to be careful, or her costumes would start getting too tight.

"I hear you and Sol are getting' married?" Brady said, as he lit a cigarette.

"Yes," Wanda said slowly. "I think so."

"Whadaya' mean, ya' think so?"

"Well, Sol and I have some things to iron out first."

"Like what, Sis?"

"Like whether I can resume my career when we return to Vegas."

"Where ya' goin'?"

"We're going to Tahiti on a cruise ship. We'll get married by the Captain."

"Wow! That sounds great!" Then he replied soberly, "But I'm not surprised Sol wants you to retire. You know, Sis, no man wants his woman lusted after by other men."

Wanda waved at him impatiently. "Oh, for Pete's sakes. It happens whether I'm on stage or in a drug store. Men always want what they don't have. Sol will just have to get used to it."

"I for one understand where he's comin' from." Brady said.

Iris took a sip of her tea. "If anyone asked me, I'd say that Wanda is a wonderful example for the rest of us who want to become more independent."

Wanda put her arm around her little sister.

Brady nodded. "Independent is good, but most men want to feel that their woman can lean on them. They want to protect them against the dogs out there."

"Thanks, little brother, for your lesson on men. I'll take your advice under consideration." Wanda made a face at Brady.

Suzanne came down the hall in her bathrobe, yawning. "What time is it?" She sauntered over to the pot and poured a cup of strong, several-hours-old coffee.

"It's two in the afternoon," Wanda said, looking at her watch. "What kept you out so late last night?"

"I was gambling at the slots until five. Didn't even realize how late it was." She turned around and saw Brady sitting at the table, just as she took a sip. Startled, she dripped coffee on her chin. "Oh! Sorry! I didn't know you had company."

Wanda laughed. "Brady's not company. He's our brother. Brady, this is my roommate, Suzanne."

He appraised the lovely woman with disheveled hair and coffee on her face. He stood and offered his hand. "Hi. Glad to meet you."

Suzanne looked at the large, brown hand in front of her. Glancing up, she stared straight into dark, intense eyes. A hint of a smile hovered around Brady's lips.

She finally took his hand with her free one. "Hello." Then her hand went immediately to her hair. "Sorry, I must look a mess. Ah…excuse me, a minute." She backed out of the kitchen and headed for her room, coffee cup still in her hand.

Brady returned to his seat. Wanda and Iris both laughed.

"Suzanne's pretty shy," Wanda said. "Doesn't let anyone but us girls see her unless she looks like she stepped from a fashion magazine."

"She's pretty beautiful just like that," Brady said, finishing his beer.

"Yes, Suzanne is beautiful, but it can be a liability for some people," Wanda said as she put out knives and forks.

Iris filled four plates with food and placed them on the table. "Dinner's ready, Suzanne," she called.

Suzanne came back into the kitchen, this time in slacks and blouse, with her hair combed and tied back in a ponytail. She had no makeup on, and Brady thought she was gorgeous. He smiled at her several times over the chicken and gravy.

"Suzanne, what kind of work do you do here in Vegas?" Brady asked.

"I work as a showgirl in the *Las Vegas Follies*," she replied.

"What does that involve? Do you dance on stage?"

"No, I mostly just walk around the stage with a huge

headdress on my head. I would love to get a dancing gig, but apparently I'm too tall for a dancer in the shows."

Brady was mesmerized; he would definitely have to get to know this wonderful creature. She probably had tons of boyfriends and wouldn't even consider going out with an Indian. Besides, he could hardly keep himself in cigarettes, let alone take this woman out on a date in Las Vegas.

Suzanne was intrigued with Wanda and Iris's brother. He was a handsome man and seemed the very opposite of Alan. Brady exuded a raw animal sexuality, which both attracted her and frightened her. She tried keeping her eyes down, but every time she looked up, his intense gaze met hers.

Brady, realizing the futility of their ever getting together, sank into a self-absorbed mood. He could dream about her, anyway.

Suzanne

After the last show, Suzanne changed, removed her stage makeup, and left the El Morocco heading across the street for the Dunes. She took a seat and started pouring silver dollars into the slot. Each time the machine kicked out a few dollars, her mouth would salivate and her pupils grew larger. She was experiencing a rush every bit as much as Alan did when he snorted coke. Her heart raced, and her nostrils flared like a thoroughbred coming up on the home stretch. She wanted to cash a personal check at the cashier's cage, but she had done that every night this week, and she was not sure how much money she had left in her account.

Reluctantly, she left the casino and headed for her car, just as dawn was breaking over the mountains. By the time she slipped into her parking place she was coming down off the high. She tried to slip her key in the lock quietly so as not to wake Iris on the couch, but when she closed the door, Iris opened her eyes and lifted her head.

"You okay, Suzanne? Wanda's been real upset."

Suzanne rubbed her eyes. "I'm fine. I told her I wouldn't be home right away."

Just then, Wanda came out of the bedroom, tying the belt of her robe. "Where the hell have you been, Suzanne? I was about to call the police." She stormed into the living room.

"I...I said I'd be late. You didn't have to worry." Suzanne spoke softly, intimidated by Wanda's anger.

"There's late, and there's daylight. Christ! It's 8 o'clock! I was afraid something had happened to you." Wanda sat on the arm of the green chair.

"I'm sorry. I didn't mean to worry anyone."

Wanda looked carefully at her roommate. "You haven't been to the high-roller parties, have you?"

Suzanne shook her head. "No, I told you, I was gambling at the Dunes.

"You've been gambling every night since Alan left. How much money have you lost?"

"I'm not sure." Suzanne looked at the rug.

"Go to bed. You've been sleeping until almost showtime. You haven't taken a dance class since he left, and you missed two rehearsals. You've got to get yourself together, girl."

Suzanne nodded. "I know." Tears sprang to her eyes. "I'm trying," she said as she moved past Wanda.

Wanda reached out and pulled Suzanne inside the circle of her arms. They stood for a moment while Suzanne cried on her shoulder.

She would have to talk to Sol about Suzanne, thought Wanda. She was ruining her life.

Iris turned over and went back to sleep.

Suzanne finally pulled away and shuffled down the hall to her room, heavy with the terrible emptiness in her heart.

Epilogue

Boise, Idaho

$\mathcal{A}$ woman with long, dark hair stepped from her new Ford and unlocked large double doors of a white, single-story building. Once inside, she flicked on the outside neon lights. A red and blue glow lit up the sign by the street: *THE RENDEZVOUS* —*Boise's most exclusive dinner club.*

She began turning on lights inside. The kitchen was lit, and the cooks were busy with the evening's preparations. She walked to her office, sat down at the desk, picked up the phone, and checked her messages. She wrote down a few numbers, then hung up, and gazed at the opposite wall. Her beautiful violet eyes focused on a picture. It was of herself with a handsome man standing in front of a large house with turrets on each end of the roof. They had their arms around each other and were smiling. The woman's eyes teared as they always did when she looked at that photograph. She missed Nick so much. She took a tissue from the pocket of her purple velvet dress as a knock sounded at the door.

"Come in," she said, quickly wiping her eyes.

The head chef appeared in his white apron and tall hat. "Evening, Miss Sky. Just wanted to remind you of the party of ten tonight. I made sure we have enough of everything to serve them.

"Thanks, Chet. I'll be out in a minute."

He closed the door, and Viola Sky went to the mirror and proceeded to wind her long hair into the usual bun she wore every night at her restaurant. She picked up the tinted glasses and put them on. They were dark enough that no one would notice the color of her eyes.

Reno, Nevada

$\mathcal{M}$rs. Phillips held her new baby in her arms. The nurse had showed her how to breast feed, and James Phillips was taking to it quite well. Just as he started to fuss, she held him to her shoulder and patted him on the back. A large man with a taxi logo on his cap entered the hospital room.

"Honey, look. He took to my breast like an old pro." The new mother laughed.

The man leaned down and kissed his son on the top of his bald head. "He's no dummy. I probably gave him some lessons while he was in the womb."

"Oh…silly," she said to her husband, then returned her attention to the baby. "He's so beautiful." She cradled the baby, teasing his mouth with her nipple. James didn't respond, preferring to close his eyes and take a nap. "I guess he's had enough," she said.

"The new house is ready to move into," Craig said. "The furniture was delivered yesterday, and I did my best to put everything in its place."

"Oh, darling, I can hardly wait to see it. Did you get the nursery ready for James?"

"Of course I did. I even stacked all his baby clothes that we bought in the drawers." Craig kissed his wife on the cheek. "I'm so proud of you, Ruby. Thank you for our baby."

She turned her head to catch his lips. "Thank you, my love, for everything."

Great Exuma, the Bahamas

*T*all and tanned, Myron Stein climbed onto his 35-foot sloop, THE SHOWGIRL, ready for a day on the bay. A local man, Peter, was his only crew. Before boarding, Pete removed all but two deck lines, bow and stern. Then he came aboard and checked the fuel and oil levels before starting the engine.

Myron went immediately below and put a block of ice, sandwiches and Scotch in the ice chest. Back on deck, he stared across the vast turquoise sea. Gulls glided just above the smooth water, and pelicans gulped fish unlucky enough to come to the surface. The clear, blue sky became a lovely backdrop for the various vessels in the harbor: a couple of nineteenth-century square riggers, numerous sloops, ketches, and cabin cruisers, several catamarans and a few house boats.

The sun warmed his body, but his heart still ached for her. In the eighteen months since he had exiled himself, she was the first thought he had each day. Even the lovely, brown-skinned Eva, who cleaned and cooked and wrapped her smooth limbs around his body at night, could not take away his loss. Sol had visited three times, his parents once. True to their word, Sol and his father kept him in plenty of cash. He had to endure his father's wrath for his exiled position, but two trips to Europe, one to Saint Moritz and twice to Paris, had helped assuage his boredom. But his days on the island were solitary and lonely. He'd taken up painting and had many canvases of the sea stacked around his place, none of them very good, he suspected.

The house where he lived had shuttered windows and grass matting on the floor. It was comfortably furnished in a casual décor. There were four bedrooms, three never used except when Sol and his parents visited together. He'd gotten used to sharing quarters with insects and geckos.

As he waited for the familiar sight of the fishing boat he met each month off the coast, trading a suitcase of money for a bag of high grade uncut cocaine, he gazed across the bay to a small atoll, wearing a small fluffy cloud like a crown. Where was she and what was she doing at this moment?

Tarzana, California

*T*he slim, beautiful blonde stepped from her convertible and entered the building through the back entrance. Out front on the window, MISS SUZANNE'S DANCE SCHOOL, was printed in black lettering. A block away, freeway traffic thundered across the land as commuters made their way into Los Angeles through the San Fernando Valley.

The young woman unlocked the front door, went to her office, changed into a white leotard and tights, slipped on white ballet shoes, and went out to the studio. Several small children between eight and ten were just coming in the front entrance.

She thanked God every day for Sol Wolfe and the way he rescued her from the pain of addiction. She had gone through her entire savings and lost her job at the El Morocco by the time Irving Samuels had picked her up and physically transported her home to Tarzana, and her parents. She had recovered there, and with the money from an anonymous donor who she was sure was Sol, she started her dance school. Often she felt her entire existence in Vegas was like a nightmare/dream that had happened a long time ago. She now lived with her parents, and they continued to be very supportive. She loved teaching and got a certain amount of satisfaction from knowing that several of her girls would go on to become dancers. It was certainly different here, from Vegas, so much healthier. She even had a boyfriend.

The ringing of the phone interrupted her thoughts. "Miss Suzanne's Dance School," she answered.

"Hi, honey." Brady's voice came over the line.

Suzanne smiled. "Hi, yourself."

"Whatcha' doin' tonight?"

"Nothing much. Why?"

"Wanna' go to a movie?"

Suzanne paused, then said, "Sure, why not? Got something in mind?"

"Oh, baby, I've always got something in mind with you. How 'bout a pizza and a movie, then spend the night at my place?"

Suzanne smiled again. "Sounds good to me."

"What time does your class end?"

"Six."

"Pick you up at six-fifteen, Okay?"

"Okay, tire man." Suzanne hung up. She thought of how successfully Brady has made the transition from reservation to suburban life. He was manager of a tire store in Reseda. She was happy with him in her life and felt content and secure in this time and place. She rarely even thought of Alan anymore.

Raiatea, Tahiti, 1976

*W*anda sat up on the blanket and watched the waves break across the Tahitian reef. So much had happened in the past year. Violet and Ruby had disappeared, and Wanda assumed they were living new lives under different names. She had been in touch with Suzanne in Southern California. Brady, too. Sol had seen Alan several times. Iris was content making a good living in Vegas, selling her prized baskets from the reservation. Her oldest sister, Naomi, remained on the reservation with Jackson, vowing never to leave. Three of them had assimilated. That was a pretty good record.

She and Sol had resolved the problem of her continued career on the stage. One day he came to her and said, "Honey, you can keep your career if you want. I'll just have to enforce respect from my peers if anyone gives me a problem."

Realizing right then that a stage career was no longer important, and she didn't want Sol to "enforce" respect from his acquaintances, she gladly gave up dancing. She admitted to herself, if not to him, that the applause no longer brought a rush, and the entire experience had lost its magic. She chalked it up to…been there, done that. She realized and admitted that Sol was the best thing that had ever happened to her, and she no longer had anything to prove to herself or her public. What more could a woman want? Well, maybe something to do when they finished traveling, she thought. Maybe teach dance like Suzanne was doing.

She glanced back at Sol coming through the open door of the grass hut with snorkels and flippers in hand. He ran across the sand, kicking up a spray, his muscular body tanned and flexible.

"Hey, Mrs. Wolfe, are you ready? We can swim out to that reef with the chartreuse fish." He threw her gear down on the blanket.

Wanda put on her top, tying the strings behind her neck. "I love those beautiful green fish," she said. "When we get home maybe we could have a tropical-fish tank? What do you think?"

"I think your wish is my desire, love, but we may not be home for a very long time," he said, laughing.

"Where are we going after this?"

"I told you we were going around the world. Tomorrow we fly to Hong Kong for a week: Then on to Singapore and Bangkok. After that, you can decide our next destination." He pulled her up and kissed her, her skin warm against his chest.

She picked up her snorkel and flippers, slipped them on in shallow water, and drove into the clear turquoise sea.

"Bet I can beat you to the reef," she called over her shoulder.

And Sol knew she probably would.

To order additional copies of this
book: www.colleenraesnovels.com
or www.createspace.com/4712718